MW01135499

Barb & Victor,

Thank you for your wonderful
help on this book, and thank you
especially for your friendship.
May God keep you
close.

Bob

GETTING OLDER

A Novel about One Senior's Fear of
Aging and Joy at Growing Old

ROBERT BAILOR

authorHOUSE®

AuthorHouse™
1663 Liberty Drive
Bloomington, IN 47403
www.authorhouse.com
Phone: 833-262-8899

© 2020 Robert Bailor. All rights reserved.

No part of this book may be reproduced, stored in a retrieval system, or
transmitted by any means without the written permission of the author.

This is a work of fiction. Names, characters, businesses, places, events and incidents
are either the products of the author's imagination or used in a fictitious manner. Any
resemblance to actual persons, living or dead, or actual events is purely coincidental.

Published by AuthorHouse 09/14/2020

ISBN: 978-1-7283-7242-6 (sc)
ISBN: 978-1-7283-7241-9 (e)

Print information available on the last page.

Any people depicted in stock imagery provided by Getty Images are models,
and such images are being used for illustrative purposes only.
Certain stock imagery © Getty Images.

This book is printed on acid-free paper.

Because of the dynamic nature of the Internet, any web addresses or links contained in
this book may have changed since publication and may no longer be valid. The views
expressed in this work are solely those of the author and do not necessarily reflect the
views of the publisher, and the publisher hereby disclaims any responsibility for them.

DEDICATION

This book is dedicated to all those confronted with growing old.
Its purpose is to suggest that being older is not
to be feared but to be embraced
in terms of a life stage marked with the opportunity
to spread unconditional love.

TABLE OF CONTENTS

PREFACE

I have been fascinated with growing old. Not with counting the passing of days, but with what getting older means. If Aristotle is right and time is really the marking of change, then to understand getting older involves an appreciation of the fact that we are marked with change. Obviously, when we are older we are different than when we were younger. Change is built into what it means to be human. So we speak of personal development, the ebb and flow of how I am me and how I relate to everything and everyone else. When I think of getting older, I think in terms of development, and from what I can see, human development does not end when we become "all grown up." Adulthood itself develops. I see adulthood as more like a new platform for development. And this is where the notion of being a senior comes in. To best understand getting older is to recognize that adulthood is itself nothing more than one stage on life's way. And since we continue to mature through adulthood, seniority can be seen as an arc that can lead to a more complete way of living as an adult.

When thinking about growing old, there are two key questions that need to be answered: Is my death the only thing to look forward to with my adulthood? Or, is my getting older really change heading toward a more complete level of human life--full maturity? It is fair to ask whether "senior citizens" are adults who are merely declining in their ability to live as adults or are people poised to be ready to move on to a fuller stage of maturity and prowess. In fact, could being advanced in years be seen as an opportunity to look beyond mere adulthood rather than a condition marked by the final death throes of life? Perhaps with the survival needs and duties of adulthood having been achieved by many seniors, they now are less distracted from what is useful and pulled toward what is fulfilling. Could it be that "end-of-life issues" become prominent for seniors precisely because they have the time and life experience to come to terms with the ultimate meaning of their lives in the face of a literal deadline?

Could being an elder be a prospect that should be embraced rather than feared? How much more exciting and enriching would growing older be if it were approached as a discovering of one's true north and a coming to personal fulfillment with the joy this brings, rather than figuring out how to get through the days, perhaps even fearfully anticipating deterioration and death.

Perhaps getting old is often seen in a negative light because it means the loss of youthful characteristics. But no adult wishes to return to infancy. Getting old brings wisdom and skill and opportunity not available with youth and all its challenges and disappointments. Maybe advancing in years should be celebrated rather than run from, because it includes the sum of experiences and insights that have already been integrated into a person's life, experiences and insights that the young, precisely because of their youth, have no access to at all. Already there are cultures where elders have embraced this mindset, the Japanese and Native Americans come to mind. But for some people the "golden years" are merely a euphemism for the "age of obsolescence."

It is with these thoughts in mind that I have written this book. There have been numerous non-fiction books written about getting older. They are good books filled with relevant facts and insights. But there is a real difference between knowing about growing old and living it, just as there is a qualitative difference between thinking about how to play a guitar and being able to play one. This book is offered as a way to appreciate getting older as lived rather than observed. It is about one person's lived experience of being a senior presented on multiple levels. The main character, Don, is living the experience of growing old while Michael is counseling him in real time about his issues with it. Entering into Don's experience of being older requires engaging his interactions with Michael, his thoughts and feelings revealed through his journal, and short stories that are really lengthy anecdotes prompted by Don's experience as he works out his day-to-day life as a septuagenarian.

That is why this book is different than a professional study on the elderly. It dives into the experience of growing old, what it feels like, what it calls a person to, what challenges are involved, so that readers can perhaps re-evaluate their own perspective on getting older. It is like being taken along by the musical flow of a symphony without thinking about who wrote it or what type of symphony it is. Reflection comes later. Like Don you will be virtually immersed in the experience of becoming a senior, and perhaps by this you will be led to a fuller and better way of approaching getting older for yourself.

Age is not a number but a state of mind.

Michael Balter, PhD, PCC

Part I: Chapter One

(THE CALL TO COUNSELING)

I guess it all started when I stayed with my son and his family for the Christmas holidays last year. Don't get me wrong. We all had a great time eating, laughing and doing the typical things that come with families getting together. The problem was that there was something missing, and we all felt it.

You see, my wife had died of ovarian cancer the previous January, and, man!, was that tough. She was a real trooper through it all. She fought it with surgery and chemo, but then the chemo became too much, and she chose to live her life to the fullest till the inevitable end.

She lasted two years without the chemo. They were very good years. Since we knew we didn't have much time left, we celebrated the time we had like we were newlyweds. We went out to plays and ballets and concerts as often as we could. We even went on a Caribbean cruise and took a tour of the whole continent of Europe. Those were things we always wanted to do but put off because of other responsibilities and because we were always saving, just in case. Well, the just-in-case was upon us, so we indulged like never before. We splurged on ourselves because we wanted to get the most we could out of the time we had left.

But the shadow of her cancer hung over us like a wet blanket. One day I caught her silently weeping as she sat by the bay window looking out at the spring flower buds and the tiny new leaves. I put my arms around her and kissed her gently on her forehead.

"I know, Sweetheart, I know. But we can get through this together. You know I'm here for you. And so are our children. Keep the faith, my Love. We'll try to make the best of it till ..."

And that's when she looked up at me with her tear-stained cheeks and said, "Till … I'm no longer here. Donnie, you know full well I believe there is an afterlife, and I believe that God is merciful. But I'm still scared. I'm going away into uncharted territory, and I'm not sure I'm strong or brave enough to see it through."

"Joannie, you're the strongest and bravest person I've ever known." My chest began to heave with grief. "We have to trust in God and trust in ourselves. We need to believe we can turn these lemons into lemonade."

Then she stood up, turned to me, and pressed herself against me as if she were trying to melt into my soul. I felt a deep sadness, but I also felt empowered by this lovely lady who was entrusting me with her destiny. How I hoped I would be worthy of that trust!

It wasn't too long after that when Joannie took a turn for the worst. She lost her strength and began to waste away. How miserable I felt! Here was my one true love slipping away from me—and I couldn't do anything about it, except to be there for her as much as I could to strengthen her and take away her fears.

I called hospice and we set up a mini hospital in our bedroom. When the time came, I phoned Alex and Mary and asked them to come home to be with their mom for her last days. They came; they wept; they told their mother how much they loved her. They hid from their mother how devastated they were, but they cried on my shoulder, and I now had three people that needed my strength.

We held on till the day when we were sitting around Joannie's bed just making small talk when suddenly she sat up and reached out her arms as if to embrace someone in the room. But it wasn't us. With a breathless and breaking voice she called out, "I'm coming, Mom and Dad." Then she laid back down and reached up to the three of us. I grasped one hand; the children grasped the other. She smiled and with her last breath whispered, "I love you all."

Then she let go. Her last breath left her, and so did her spirit. I thought I saw a cloud-like haze rise from her body, and then I knew she was no longer there.

You know, I have to stop talking about this now or I'll be no good for the rest of the day. So if you don't mind, I'll tell you why I decided to go see Michael.

As I now think about it, it seemed to begin before that Christmas visit. After Joannie's death everything on the outside seemed just fine, but the emptiness I felt within seemed to spread to every corner of my soul. Yes, I laughed with the family, and, yes, I played with little Abby and made her giggle. But as the time wore on, the joy I had felt at the beginning of the visit wore off only to be replaced by a sense of duty to my family and a feeling of getting through the day rather than embracing it.

You see, this new feeling was all about how I was feeling about my future. Slowly but surely a sense of weariness was overtaking me. It wasn't the sense that I had nothing to look forward to; it was the feeling that there was no reason to look forward to anything in the first place.

I had retired from the job I loved as a high school history teacher in order to spend as much time as I could with Joannie. Before she got sick, I had expected to continue on as a teacher till "I would slump over my podium because I simply ran out of steam." But I couldn't leave Joannie all alone at home with the cancer.

So I retired with no plans for the future except to spend as much time as possible with Joannie. And now that she was gone, I saw no plans in the works. Sure I had children to care for and grandchildren to play with, but that somehow did not seem enough to get my butt out of bed every morning.

After Joannie died, I came to realize that I was in my early 70's, I was without a job, and I was basically all alone in a big, beautiful house that every day reminded me of what I no longer had. I know I shouldn't have, but I began to isolate myself. Not on purpose, but because I lacked purpose. Friends and former colleagues called, but I told them all that I had other plans, but of course I didn't. I didn't want to join any organizations because I lacked the energy to start new projects. I didn't want to get involved with my church because I didn't want to talk about Joannie's death, nor did I want to work with "old people," the demographic that seemed to be the biggest group of volunteers at the parish.

Mary and Alex both called me regularly and we enjoyed sharing our thoughts and our feelings, but the conversations always somehow got around to their mother, and that depressed me. Soon when they realized that I wasn't leaving my house except on Sundays for church, they began to give me advice about what I should be doing with my life. Now, don't get me wrong, I appreciated their concern and I took into consideration their suggestions and their warnings about what I was doing to myself. But they did not, could not, understand what I was going through. I felt a deep emptiness about my life and a searing question about whether that emptiness extended forward to my future. These feelings spread like a cancer that grabbed hold of the very way I approached my entire life.

You see, I had always been a rather optimistic kind of guy. I took life as it came and tried to make the best of even tough situations. I looked forward to my days just to see what surprises and blessings each day held. But now I felt hopeless and helpless. I couldn't get myself going to meet the day. What was the use? I no longer had my Joannie and I no longer had my students. What was there to live for?

I know. I know. Those are the kind of thoughts that get my demographic into trouble. Isolation, depression, ennui. Bad combination, dangerous, in fact. But that was my life. I seemed to be weighed down by them, and I did not seem to have the strength to get up and fight them.

I guess things were getting a bit out of hand when out of the blue my son said he was in town for business and wondered if I had time for some lunch. That seemed like a good break from my daily routine of drinking coffee in the morning and drinking beer in the evening till I tramped off to bed. So we decided to meet at Barney's where they served that pot roast like Joannie used to make. I must admit, I was a little anxious that Alex would bring up my do-nothing life, but I figured I could weather any criticism he might make because I would be with someone I loved who was still here.

When I walked into the restaurant, Alex was already there in a quiet corner booth. This, of course, worried me a bit because it seemed like a set-up, but I didn't want to spoil the moment and thanked him for taking care of things.

When the waitress came over and asked if we wanted anything to drink before we ordered, Alex looked at me and said, "Don't worry about it, Dad. This lunch is on me."

I replied with a smile on my face, "Well, if that's the case, I'll start with one of those 22-ouncers on special today." Alex ordered the same and we settled in to be with each other.

Alex started with, "So, how you doin', Dad?"

I knew he would begin with a question like that, and I was prepared for it.

"I'm doin' OK. Got enough to eat, house is warm, and the car is running fine."

Alex knew I was trying to skirt the real meaning of his question. "That's not what I meant, Dad. I mean, how are you feeling? The last time we spoke on the phone, or should I say, the last time I spoke to you, you didn't have much to say. And when you did speak you sounded so weary."

I tried hard to get out of the corral Alex was putting me in. "I was a little tired that day. No big deal." The waitress came with our beers and just dropped them off seeing how we were deep in conversation.

After we both took our first hearty drink from the pilsners, Alex renewed his persistent search for my real condition. "Dad, it is a big deal. Mary and I have talked about your situation, and we're worried about you. You're not yourself lately. It's like you're only going through the motions with your life. You know, I can't remember when the last time was I heard you belly laugh like you used to. I love you, Dad, and I don't want to lose you too."

That statement hit me hard, and I began to tear up. "Alex, I won't let you lose me. I've been going through a rough patch lately. You know I buried my bride of forty-eight years and I gave up teaching to be with her till the end. So, what am I left with?"

I paused realizing that I had implied that Alex, Mary and their families were of little consequence to me. That's not what I meant at all. So I tried to explain myself without hurting Alex. "Son, I didn't mean to imply that there's no one and nothing left for me. I still have you and Mary and your wonderful families. You all mean the world to me. What I meant was that with your Mom gone and teaching out of my life, I'm having a real problem with figuring out what the meaning of my life is right now. It's this sense of being lost that has thrown me for a loop. I feel sad and tired and confused all at once. I really appreciate how you and Mary and even the kids have been by my side, trying to cheer me up and show me how wonderful life can be. It's just getting harder and harder for me to see how life can be wonderful anymore. I'm feeling old and used up and ready for the trash heap. It's like I'm just waiting to die because then I'll be with your mother again."

Alex reached over the table and put his hand on mine. "I can't know exactly what you're going through, Dad, but I know I love you, and if you're hurting, I'm hurting. It's just like, remember when we lost the championship football game and I was really down in the dumps? What did you do? You ran on that field as if we had won and you threw your arms around me and told me you couldn't be more proud of me. The game may have been a loss, but I--I was definitely a winner."

"You know that changed my whole perspective on the game. You know that I didn't play football in college because I blew out my knee, but I didn't see myself as a loser ever again. That's why I was able to get through law school and raise a beautiful family like you did us."

Alex paused and choked up with sincerity. "Dad, you're a winner too. In fact you're my hero. And I want you to know that I'm going to go through with you whatever it takes to get my ol' father back, because I miss him."

I was deeply touched. My son whom I took care of was now taking care of me. How ironic, but how wonderful! I asked, "What do you suggest?"

Alex smiled and replied, "I know about this guy. His name in Michael Balter. He's a fulltime philosophy professor but he's also a part-time counselor. And I hear he's really good. Best of all he specializes in people like you who seem to have lost their way in life."

"How do I get in contact with him?"

"Not to worry. I just happen to have his phone number and address right here in my pants pocket."

"Of course you do," I noted with no surprise but with plenty of gratitude.

Alex gave me the piece of paper and I tucked it into my shirt pocket for easy access. I looked across the table with glassy eyes and said, "Thank you, Alex. Thank you very much."

We sat silently for a short while then until the waitress reappeared and asked us if we were ready to order. I exclaimed enthusiastically, "We sure are! I think I'll take one of everything on the menu."

Alex laughed at this remark and added, "Now that's my Dad!"

We ordered and ate and laughed and bonded like never before. It was a good day that showed me a glimmer of escape out of my gloom. When we finished eating, we hugged each other and went our separate ways. As soon as I got home, I called Michael and made my first appointment.

Part I: Chapter Two

(THE FIRST COUNSELING SESSION)

I looked wistfully out of the office window at the massive oak tree with its leaves slowly falling to the ground. *If these are my Autumn days, what do I have to look forward to in my Winter days?* I was talking to myself and rudely ignoring the young man who was sitting quietly across from me with clipboard and pen in hand.

I growled at him, "Getting old sucks! I see some pretty damn disturbing things happening to me! The hair on my head is greying, and what's left is falling out. Age spots come from nowhere and freckle my skin. Random hair pops up all over my body, and I'm now wearing trifocals. I get tired quicker too. And when I manage to rev up my willpower, even my willpower starts to sputter. Add to this that I seem to need more sleep, I'm not that hungry anymore, and I like having a blanket over my legs when I read or watch TV. Should I go on?"

Michael's gaze was fixed on my face, but I could tell he was not judging me. Instead he seemed to be trying to understand and empathize with what I was saying and feeling. With a soft, encouraging voice he replied, "Keep going. I'm listening."

I thought, *what do I have to lose?* So I felt free to go on sharing my thoughts and feelings, glad to be able to vent. "What's more, I can't remember things like I used to. When I have to recall a name or a date or something-or-other, I have to rummage through my memory only to come up with a blank. Then, bam!, while I'm doing something totally different, all at once I remember what I wanted to recall an hour ago. And, I hate to say this, but, you know, I even go stretches when I don't care about sex. It's not that I'm bored with it. It's simply that sex doesn't interest me that much anymore. For the past few years I've even wondered whether I was up to it. More and more my performance was frustrating and embarrassing, if you know what I mean."

My eyes became glassy, and I spoke to Michael as if I were letting him in on a secret, "I can certainly understand how people my age begin to think that their best days are over. The present is just something to get through. The future is more of the same, or worse."

I sat back in the stuffed chair across from Michael and looked at him to see whether I had made any sense. Then I blurted out, "You see why I need some help with this, can't you? But at least I'm not the only one thinking like this. It seems that everyone my age is thinking the same way. At parties and seminars, even in prayer groups, it seems like the conversation comes around sooner or later to feeling old and missing our younger selves. Our common fear is that we are living on a downward slope ending in death. It's slippery, and we have to figure out how to hold on to the guard rails or we'll slide into a void of pain and paralysis."

Michael sat back in his chair next to the floor lamp and said, "Thank you for being so honest, Don. I would be more than happy to work with you on this, especially the depression I see coloring everything you have told me. As you say, you're not the only one trying to work through growing old. I'm hoping our meetings will teach us both the best way to navigate this stage of life. I believe I can learn from you just as much as you can learn from me. I may be the professional here, but you clearly are the person full of life's wisdom."

Michael paused for a second, then went on. "We may be ending our talk here, but the counseling must go on. So if you don't mind I would like to give you something to do at home. Would you be willing to keep a journal of your daily thoughts and feelings? This will help you become aware of where you are and can help you get started taking on the challenges you're faced with. Perhaps we can use your entries as jumping-off points for our next sessions."

"Okay. I'll give this journaling a shot. It certainly beats watching game shows and old movie reruns."

Michael stood up and extended his hand to me. I stood and put out my hand to shake his. And as our hands came together, Michael cupped my hand in both of his. Honestly, I was caught off guard by that gesture, but then I began to see it as a pledge to work with me no matter what that meant. I felt encouraged by his concern and embarrassed by my own hesitation.

"Shall we meet same time, same place next week?" Michael asked.

"How about if I call you about when a good time would be?" I replied. "I want to take you up on that journal thing, and I'm not sure when I'll be ready to share it with you. When it feels right to me, I'll give you a call."

"Sounds good to me. You know, you did very well today, Don. Your honesty was refreshing and revealing. You seem like the kind of person I would like to get to know better. So until next time. Peace!"

Michael let go of my hand. Then I picked up my windbreaker and headed for the door. But before I went out, I turned and gestured a "thumbs up" to Michael, and Michael smiled back.

Part II: Chapter One

(JOURNAL ENTRIES #1 & #2)

Journal Entry #1

Do I need counseling? I can't tell for sure, but I figure it can't hurt, and as I get older I think more and more about what I'm missing—and that brings me down. I guess it's better to nip the blues in the bud before I run off the track and do something stupid.

So, I've decided to follow Michael's advice and think about what growing old means and what it has to do with me, my future, how it all turns out. I'll be talking to you, journal, about how I came to be the way I am, and I'll share some of what I write in you with Michael. I really prefer to talk it out rather than write it out, but it couldn't hurt and maybe I can capture my thoughts and feelings before they ride off into the sunset and disappear like so many scattered dreams.

I guess my concern with getting older began when I found my first white hair when I was sixteen. I was getting ready for the day, and when I looked at myself in the bathroom mirror, I spied that little sucker because it was taunting me, springing out of my thick black crop of hair and daring me to pay attention to it. Well, you know what I did? I got a pair of tweezers and I pulled it out. How dare it taunt me that way? I was too young to have white hair. That was the old-man-me a million years in the future, not the young-man-me with a destiny that I was happy and ready to work hard on. I had so much to look forward to. I knew I was smart and talented, and not too bad looking either. All I had to do was work hard, and a good life would be mine. Yet that one white hair mocked my hopes. It brought to my mind that all I work for might not happen because I'm just me, and the world will have its say no matter how I go about my life. It's remembering that one white hair that has brought me to where I am now. Maybe my 70's is what that hair was really all about.

But it's not just that white hair. It's my head of grey hair (what's left of it) and the feeling that what that white hair implied is what I'm living through right now. Is it the end game of my life?

Well, I have to stop this, because it's only making me tired and blue. So maybe I should think this through carefully. But I hate to write. Never kept a journal in my life. Still, I'm paying the man big bucks to help me through all this, so maybe I should give it a try. I'll keep this journal till Michael and I meet again. No specific date. I'll call him back when I'm ready. I think I'll be ready soon, but who knows?

I will call these reflections *My Aging Journal*. No, that sounds too much like my last will and testament. How about *My Thoughts about Getting Older*? Better. Ponder and write; write and ponder.

It wasn't so bad to do this one. Too long-winded, though. I'll get better with time and practice.

Journal Entry #2

Today I was passing by a mirror and with the corner of my eye I saw--my father. Scary thought. Funny thing that we never knew our parents as young people. They're always "older." And we never give it a thought that they probably experienced exactly what we're experiencing now. Did my dad have trouble with growing older too? I'll never know. But he still loved me and worked hard so my life would turn out even better than his. I wonder if the experience of growing old has to do more with an attitude than a calendar.

But I digress. How should I begin my story? Since my future is determined by my present and my present is determined by my past, I guess the key to my future is my past. But, then again, maybe not. Doesn't my thinking about my past change the way I see myself in the present? So maybe it's my approach to my present that determines my future, not my past at all. It's confusing yet engrossing. But enough with these thoughts. On with the facts.

I'm an overall healthy and successful 73-year-old. Same me, just different ways of doing things. Same fears, same abilities, same likes. When you look at me, you probably see "an old man." But it's the same me inside. Sometimes I get confused by my outward appearance. Who is that elderly guy looking back at me in the mirror? It can't be me--but it is. When I look at a picture of me in my earlier years, I see a striking difference. But that's on the outside! Inside I feel a lot like I did when those pictures were taken, or even before that. I'm working out the same anxieties and fears and bad habits I had way back when. I feel like I'm the same person I was back then. Many of my "issues" bother me just like when I was younger. Then I'm sure I'm the same me, and I get angry at myself for not being a different me that can deal with my problems better. After all, I am older. Shouldn't I be wiser?

But am I really "old"? Or am I just "older"? Come to think of it, I've been older than I was yesterday every day other than the first day I ever lived. Is this any different?

Haven't worked through it all yet. I thought that when I got to this age I would have it all together, be living on a plateau, easy street. But it's not like that. I guess it couldn't be like that because I've gone through some things that come with age and were only hinted at when I was younger.

Like my retirement. I liked my work as a high school history teacher. Was with the same school for 40 years! That is until I called it quits because of Joannie's condition. But I must admit at times the daily teaching ritual was becoming a drudgery rather than a joy. Loved the kids! But I more and more hated all that paperwork and my having to revise my classes with the new computer software.

Supported my family with that job. Sent my two kids to college. Even went on some exciting adventures. So I'm not sorry I spent all those years in that school building. But I felt that, even if Joannie had stayed in good health, I needed to wind down from my work-a-day life. My family was raised, my house paid off, my pension secured. I was finding it hard to find a reason to continue but could not pull the trigger on my moving on. Then Joannie's illness gave me the best reason in the world for retiring, to devote myself to her while there was still time.

Now I no longer have my teaching and no longer have my Joannie. There's a chasm in my heart where Joannie lived, and there's a hole in my heart where my teaching lived. With both gone I'm not sure what I have to look forward to now.

But I can't be the only one who has ever felt this way. Others must have gone through the same thing. If so, what would that look like? I can just imagine ...

Part II: Chapter Two

(DON'S STORY ABOUT RETIRING)

NOW WHAT?

The toastmaster pulled out a yellow balloon from beneath the podium with a toupee on top of it and a face drawn with black marker that looked surprisingly like Ted. The audience howled with laughter at the sight. Ted blushed with embarrassment but gave in to the jest and joined the crowd with a belly laugh.

"So now I would like to call our esteemed colleague up here to say a few words. Oh, and I'll leave his likeness next to him so we won't mistake who he is." The crowd erupted in laughter once again then settled down when Ted stepped up to the podium.

"I wish I looked that good," remarked Ted. And the audience chuckled, then quieted down out of respect and anticipation as to what the honoree would say. Ted felt unbalanced and overwhelmed. Was all this just for him? He knew he was liked at work, but did he really have these many admirers? He had prepared some remarks, but he wondered whether they fit with the levity of the situation. This was not his first time in front of an audience, but it was the first time he was ever the center of attention—and the first time he had ever retired.

Ted hesitated at first but figured it would be better to say something than to stand there like a statue and disappoint those who had done so much to show their appreciation for him. He took out a handwritten piece of paper, laid it out on the podium and looked over the entire assembly. They were looking at him intently hoping he would say something appropriate, maybe even profound. *I'm not sure I can do this*, Ted said to himself, but then he grabbed hold of the podium with both hands and began to speak, figuring anything he said was better than this awkward silence.

"I don't know what to say," he began. "You all have been so kind to me. I don't deserve this." Just then someone yelled out from the crowd, "Yes, you do!" And the assembly began to clap for Ted, which made him blush and gave him the confidence to go on.

"Thank you so very much, all of you! Here I am at the end of a long journey. Forty-two years to be exact. And I'm surrounded by my family, my friends, my co-workers, even my supervisors." The crowd chuckled at this remark.

"I've spent the biggest part of my life here at Superior Tools, and I'm glad that I have. But I have decided to move on. Not because I'm running from anything or anyone, but because I feel that my work here is done. I have been blessed with this job and the people I have worked with and laughed with. There was never a dull day at the shop." Ted's closest co-workers smiled broadly at the implications of this remark. "But every challenge, every crisis was an opportunity to make things better and to share things deeper."

Ted paused dramatically then said, "That's why no matter how I felt, I always knew you all had my back, that we would succeed together, no matter what. And so I leave with hope for the future but sadness over what is now past. My work may be over, but I am not. I am launching myself into a new adventure. And with Gloria by my side as she has been for over fifty years, I expect to enjoy a new type of life."

Although a bit choked up, Ted pressed on. "When times get tough, I will recall all that each and every one of you and this company has meant to me, and I will know that even though the past is past, the past foretells the future." His eyes glassed over. "Who knows what will become of me? But I will still be the me you see standing before you, and with your thoughts and prayers this me will not just 'ride off into the sunset,' but will ride off over the horizon into a new world of living, loving and laughing.

"Again, I'm so grateful that I have had you all in my life. I know full well that we will no longer play the same roles in each others' lives. But that doesn't mean we can't play different and exciting roles once I leave. So I'm not saying 'goodbye.' I'm saying, 'so long.' Even if we don't get together ever again, you will always be in my heart."

He bowed his head as if he were fighting back tears. Then Ted looked up and finished by saying, "For someone who is afraid to talk, I guess I can be long-winded. I need to end this talk, but I will never end what you have meant to me. Thank you for the retirement gifts. Thank you for the opportunities to make the world just a little bit better by our work. And thank you for being there with me. I couldn't have made it to this moment without you. God Bless!"

The crowd spontaneously rose to their feet and clapped enthusiastically as if to show Ted one last time how much they appreciated him. Ted sat back down with his family, the toastmaster concluded the proceedings, and people slowly filtered out of the party room. The celebration was over, but the struggle had just begun, and that is how Ted felt as he stood up to shake the hands of so many well-wishers until the room was finally empty except for him and his family.

Ted felt sad/happy. *Now what?* he thought as he drove home. *They were all there. My achievements were on full display. But now it's over. It's just Gloria and me, and I'm heading home with the thought that tomorrow I don't have to get up to go to work. I will be free. But free for what?*

That thought haunted him the whole time he was driving home. And when he walked into his house, he saw it like he had never seen it before. His home was now no longer a base of operations but the center of his life. *Was it enough? Had he done the right thing to retire? What was he now that he was no longer a skilled craftsman with a family and a company depending on him?*

After he and Gloria unloaded their car, Ted sank comfortably into his special chair, a red recliner that he watched TV in and slept in when his bed was not good enough to keep him asleep. Gloria sat across from him on a couch.

"Can I get you something, Sweetheart?" asked Gloria.

"No thank you, Love. I think I want to just sit here quietly and try to figure out what just happened."

Gloria looked surprised at this remark. "What just happened was the wonderful culmination of forty-some years of hard work and dedication. I'm surprised you're not overflowing with joy."

"I know. I know," replied Ted with a concerned look on his face. "I guess it's all too much. Especially with the fact that it's over. I keep thinking about when my father died and how I was so broken up with grief, but I didn't have the time to be sad because I had the responsibility of planning the funeral and taking care of my mom, my younger brothers and sisters, and you and the kids. But when it was all over, I cried. I went down in the basement and cried until I could cry no longer."

Ted got up from his chair, walked over to where Gloria was sitting and took her hands in his. "That's how I feel right now," he shared. "Like I've experienced the death of my old life. And now that all the celebration is over, I'm left with an empty feeling, of wondering whether there is another life ahead for me. Please don't think this has anything to do with you, Sweetheart. I know you love me and will be with me throughout what life I have left. But I'm feeling like I'm at a crossroad. That was then, but what is there now? I keep thinking that it's over and wondering what I have to look forward to. And that's the problem, Honey. Looking forward to what? Am I supposed to simply be satisfied with what has been and just rest on my laurels? That would be 'rocking chair retirement,' and that seems like waiting for death. Should my new years be a repeat of my childhood when I had nothing to do but play, play, play? Should I charge into something new? But what, what, what?"

Seeing that her husband was in distress, Gloria now pressed down on Ted's hands that were still entwined with hers and said sympathetically, "So much thinking isn't good for you, Ted, and after such a long yet happy day. Let's leave the gifts on the table and get ready for bed. Maybe in the morning with some good sleep things will look a bit different than they do now."

"You're right, Glor," Ted admitted. "But let's keep holding hands like we used to do when we were first married. I'm so happy that at least there's one thing I can be sure of when I can't fathom what my future might hold."

"What's that, Love?"

"That your hands will always be there for me."

Gloria kissed Ted gently on his forehead, and the two walked hand-in-hand up the stairs to bed.

The morning came with Ted feeling well-rested since he did not have to be jarred awake by the screech of an alarm clock. Yet even though he felt physically rested, he remained restless. He was still bothered by the questions that had disturbed him the night before. With sleep they had faded but not disappeared. Ted figured he could continue to lie in bed and let his thoughts race incoherently or he could get out of bed and try to start the day. He wondered what the day would be like since he was not pressed to get to work on time. He felt free but at a loss as to how to spend his freedom.

So Ted got out of bed and headed downstairs to make some coffee and read the morning paper as he had always wanted to do but was in too much of a hurry to get to work. His hot morning coffee soothed him but seemed to only gloss over what bothered his heart. He read the paper from cover to cover but he felt oddly disconnected to all the major stories. Ted felt somehow outside of the real world and confused about how he should feel about that.

Having finished the paper, he gazed out the kitchen window at the bright landscape that colored his backyard, the same backyard where he had played with his kids and grandkids, where he had struggled to prepare Gloria's vegetable garden in spite of the roots and rocks that resisted his best efforts, and where he and Gloria had sat quietly drinking wine and talking together about their memories and plans. Now, as he sat at the kitchen table looking out of the window, he realized he could vividly recall the many wonderful experiences he had had in that lovely setting, but he could not for the life of him come up with any prospects for that setting that he could look forward to. That unnerved him. Was he at a point in his life when there were no possibilities left? No new challenges to meet? No adventures to pursue?

Disheartened, Ted turned away from the window and went over to his red recliner and just closed his eyes trying to not think about anything anymore. But that seemed impossible. Questions kept interjecting themselves as if there were some disruptive spirits that held him fast and kept whispering ideas that served to confuse him and darken his mood.

He tried to fight against those spirits, but their power overwhelmed him. Then he found himself turning inward since it was, obviously, his own weakness that was allowing his mind to twist and turn. He said to himself, *What the hell is going on with me? I am a master tool and die maker. I have come up with specific tools and parts for some pretty sophisticated experiments. I was so skilled and creative that I became a shift foreman with 20 people reporting to me in the shop. I know how to make decisions, to manage, to solve problems, to think outside the box to get things done. Why can't I control my own thoughts and feelings? Maybe I'm not as smart or as strong as I thought I was.*

And that began a downward spiral of self-incrimination and self-doubt that began to bring up failures and errors that reached back to childhood. *For one, there was yesterday when he had been harshly short with Gloria when she called upstairs for him to hurry dressing because they might be late to the retirement party. Then there was the time he invested in a stock that looked so very promising but tanked and he lost much of the money he and Gloria were saving for a long-awaited European vacation. And there was the time he got into a fight at work that could have cost him his job if it weren't for Jason's admission that Ted pushed him and punched him in self-defense. In high school he lied when he was caught with the lunch money of an under-classman just to get out of a well-deserved suspension. And when he was 7-years-old, on Christmas day, he was "goofing around" with his Superman action figure at the dining room table and it slipped out of his hands and knocked over the beautiful red and green candle his mother had placed on the table cloth. And it burned a big hole in the tablecloth which made his mother cry since it was an heirloom from her grandmother. And, and, and …*

Ted roused himself from the chair, saw Gloria in the other room silently reading the morning paper and decided to no longer endure his pounding headache and finally take charge of the situation. He opened the door to the basement and went directly to the liquor cabinet that he and Gloria had agreed to keep away from the children. Ted picked up a small glass, filled it with ice from the nearby refrigerator and poured himself a stiff drink of bourbon. He knew the effect bourbon had on him, and he knew that it was really too early to be drinking, but *desperate times call for desperate measures.* He added some tap water to the mixture, waited a short while for the liquid to cool and blend, then pounded it down till he felt his throat constrict and his stomach flare. He then put more water into the glass and gulped it down to relieve those awful symptoms.

Now he felt better. Now he could face the day. But what did he have to face? Unwrapping the presents, yes. Having meals with Gloria, yes. Watching some of his favorite TV shows, yes. But what about the rest of the time? Ted pondered this for some time while he looked out a basement window with a view almost fully obstructed by a large decorative bush. But that did not bother him since he was not really looking out the window but into himself. *Filling time. Is that what retirement is all about?* When he was working certainly there were days when he looked at the clock hoping that his shift would be over. The job seemed endless, and he was tired and there were so many things to do. But now there was no punching in or punching out at all. There was no wishing there was more time to get things done; there was no wishing that there were less things to get done in the time he had to do them. There was only now, and the vistas of the now seemed empty. There was nothing he had to do. Nothing to achieve. Nowhere to be. It was like he was stuck in a box of meaninglessness which was terrifying. Worse yet, it seemed to have no end.

It was time to go back upstairs. He did not want Gloria to think he had dropped dead. So Ted turned from the window feeling a sadness that he resented because it was sapping away the joy that should color his retirement. He filled his glass with water, drank it to distract himself and hurriedly went back upstairs to re-enter the land of the real from the dark world he had fallen into.

"Are you OK, Honey," asked Gloria from the dining room.

"I'm fine," answered Ted, desperately trying to hide the sadness and despair that was covering him over. *Why ruin Gloria's day too?* He felt embarrassed to be so vulnerable to his own racing and menacing thoughts.

The rest of the day went as well as might be expected because Ted busied himself with his retirement gifts, looking and laughing at the many pictures and videos from the party, and helping Gloria clean the house. They decided to go out for Chinese food in the evening and then settled in for an evening of watching TV till they were ready for bed. *Well enough,* Ted felt when the time came to retire to their bedroom. *I got through today, but will tomorrow be more of the same? Surely my days can be filled, but will they be filled with boredom or excitement?* He closed his eyes to sleep although he wished he had visited the basement one more time for a little help.

Being busy, busy, that's the secret of retirement. Keeping busy, thought Ted as he drove over to his daughter's house to put handles on her kitchen cabinets. Both Ruth and Dan worked fulltime, so they had little time to complete such minor Mr. Fix-it chores. And they were in no financial shape to afford a professional handy man. So Ted volunteered to do the work. In fact, he looked forward to the task since it gave him a reason to get up that morning and something to do with his time till the evening.

The last couple of weeks had dragged on and on since all he could find to do was clean the house and get rid of the "junk" that had accumulated around the place during the years he and Gloria where raising their three kids. At first that project gave him some satisfaction because it cleared up areas of the house that had been cluttered and neglected for years. But then he got it in hand, and the trivial other stuff around the house only made him angry at having to do such menial tasks. So it was a relief when Ruth brought up the idea of his working around her house as a handyman since the house was a "fixer-upper" and needed the touch of a master craftsman, and Ted was someone who was creative and good with his hands.

Ted arrived at Ruth and Dan's house about 9 am and left about 5 pm, and throughout that time his spirits were lifted, and he felt happy since he was doing something meaningful again. He felt useful, and this revived his spirits.

And so his Mr. Fix-It role carried on for weeks and then months. Ted felt he had found a new place for himself. He no longer worked for an organization. He was an independent agent! His successes were totally his, and he had the responsibility to fix all his mistakes on his own. Ted felt proud of what he was doing and began to stop looking back at what he had given up with his retirement. He was notching some pretty significant accomplishments, plus he was helping out his family.

Ted was surprised how he took so easily to working with electricity and plumbing and carpentry work. It seemed as if he had a natural talent for working with his hands. There was a good deal of satisfaction. When he completed a project, he could see and touch what he had created.

Because his work was so good, Ted's reputation as a handyman spread, first to his other children and then to their friends and his too. The requests for his help poured in. He remodeled his children's houses to their satisfaction and delight. He rewired a couple houses for friends. He was most proud of the 3-car garage he built with his friend, Frank. He especially enjoyed working side-by-side with him on this project. More and more Ted was convinced that his retiring was a really good idea. He had launched a great adventure, and he felt younger than he looked.

But that all began to change when Ted started to lose flexibility and strength in his hands. At first he thought it was just a matter of clumsiness on his part. But it happened too often and too regularly to be just clumsiness.

He had always been sure handed before, but now he was frequently losing his grip on his tools, sometimes at critical times that led to errors and lengthy clean-ups. He had to admit that his fingers were constantly in a state of low-grade achiness.

Then one evening when he and Gloria were playing cards with some friends at their house, it happened. It was Ted's turn to deal. He picked up the scattered cards, stacked them in a single deck and began to shuffle them. But he found it hard to do. *There are so many cards,* he thought. He tried to bridge shuffle them but could not keep them together. They kept flying every which way. And as he kept trying to control them, he felt a definite stiffness in both his hands along with a slight pain as if they were cramping up. To avoid further embarrassment and to move the game along, Ted handed the stack of cards to Gloria and asked if she would be kind enough to shuffle them for him. And so it went throughout the evening, which was pleasant enough, although Ted kept feeling a slight burning in his finger joints. He asked Gloria to shuffle the cards when it was his turn, and just put the unopened wine bottle on the table announcing, "Help yourselves."

When their company left, Gloria started cleaning up and asked if he was all right.

"I couldn't shuffle the cards, Glo. What does that mean?"

Gloria looked sympathetically at Ted and replied, "It probably means we should buy an automatic shuffler." She chuckled.

But Ted did not think the remark funny at all. "It's not a laughing matter! I'm beginning to understand why I keep dropping my tools. I bet I have arthritis in both my hands, and I don't have time for that."

With loving concern writ all over her face, Gloria said, "Let's make an appointment with Dr. Seth and see what the situation is. Till then, let's enjoy the moment. We had a lovely evening. I have you and you have me. To hell with everything else."

"I know you love me, Sweetheart." He enfolded Gloria in his arms. "What I don't know is what all this means for my future." He hesitated, looked squarely in his wife's eyes and said as if he had gained confidence from her words and her nearness, "Still, there is no reason to let the future spoil the present. What I have far outweighs what I might be losing. And I cannot put into words how much I have with you." And he kissed Gloria tenderly and slipped his hand from her back to her backside and squeezed gently. Gloria readily understood what that meant. She stepped away from him slightly, grabbed his hand in hers and led him straightway to their bedroom.

Ted and Gloria went to see the doctor a week later. The diagnosis was clear and harsh. Ted had progressive, degenerative osteoarthritis for which there is no cure, just pain management. Ted was given prescriptions for various medications and advised to try some homeopathic remedies, like taking collagen supplements and applying ice packs. But Ted only heard that his condition was permanent and would only get worse.

No one spoke in the car as Ted drove home from the doctor's office. Ted was at a loss for words; Gloria was afraid to say the wrong thing. She knew that the diagnosis was not what Ted wanted to hear, and she knew that he would be sullen and silent for some time. That was his way of dealing with such foreboding news.

When Ted parked the car in the garage, he just sat and simply stared out the front window. Gloria turned to him and asked, "Are you OK, my Love?"

"I just want to sit here for a while. You go in and do what you have to do. I'll be in shortly," replied Ted.

But it was a good fifteen minutes that Ted just sat virtually frozen to his car seat. He finally got out of the car, shut the garage door and came into the house. He did not look at Gloria. He did not look at anything. He just went into the basement and opened the liquor cabinet. Ted poured himself a generous amount of bourbon and sat down in the beige lounge chair that was tucked into the corner of the furnished basement. He then began to sip the bourbon straight, something he had never done before. He was not drinking for pleasure, but for escape.

Ted was confused and angry and sad at the same time. *What does all this mean?* He thought as he sat quietly with a second glass of bourbon in his hand. *My hands are my life. What am I without them? What can I do? Why should I even try?*

But then his thoughts became darker yet. *Why is this happening to me? What did I do to deserve this? Who am I if I can't make or do or fix? Is this how I'm supposed to spend my "golden years"? Debilitated? Cramped up like some freak? Dependent on someone else to feed me and wipe my ass?"*

Then Ted wept. His weeping was deep down because it expressed his pain at the loss not only of his power but of the only self he knew. And as warm tears flowed down his cheeks, he did not pay attention to the glass of bourbon he was holding and let it fall crashing to the floor.

Gloria heard this and ran down the stairs only to find her beloved husband with his hands over his face sighing and repeating, "It can't be." She knelt in front of him, raised his head and softly enfolded his face in her hands. In a gentle and assuring manner she looked into his tearful eyes and said, "It will be OK, my Love. We'll get through this together." And she gently kissed both cheeks. But Ted did not respond. Instead he sat back and fell asleep. Disappointed but not discouraged, Gloria stood up, took a blanket from the corner of the room and placed it on Ted. She then went back upstairs and knelt in prayer for her beloved.

The next few months were the beginning of the end for Ted. He yearned to be useful, but he faced a future of uselessness. His hands were his livelihood. Without them he would be just something that exists, not helpful, not appreciated, not valued. He could not shake this mood which was more than a mood. It became his signature attitude. Ted could find nothing to smile about, nothing to get out of bed for, nothing to replenish his energy on behalf of.

So Ted stagnated. He grew weak and confused and static. Gloria was aware of this, but no matter what she did--baked his favorite desserts, took him to movies he might like, invited their friends and children to the house—nothing seemed to cheer him up. It was like he had faded from the world around him.

Every day he wore the same pajama pants and undershirt. Every day he drank coffee in the morning and bourbon at night. Every day his demeanor was sullen and his facial expression flat.

This went on till Gloria could take it no longer. So she spent more and more time out of the house. Sometimes she went on shopping dates with "the girls." Other times she went out to dinner and dancing with friends. Then sometimes she went out just by herself. She felt she was too young to fade away like Ted, who didn't seem to even care whether she stayed home or not. In fact, nothing Gloria said or did over the months since that doctor's visit seemed to make any impact on him. He was just withering away. He wished he were dead.

Then he got his wish. One day when Gloria came home late after a fun night out with friends, she found Ted in the basement in his lounge chair with a half-filled glass of bourbon on the lampstand next to the chair. She called his name. She shook him. She checked his breath and pulse. Ted was dead. A deep vein thrombosis had sealed his fate. She felt sorrow mixed with relief. He had not remained the vibrant, engaged person she had married and lived with for all those years. Since the diagnosis of his arthritis, he had virtually disappeared from the scene. It was as if he willed his own passing. She could not recognize him because he could not recognize himself.

His retirement meant the end of Ted. He had held on for a while, but then he gave up. When Gloria buried him, she felt that he was not leaving her, but she was putting him to rest, for he had lost himself.

Damn it! I don't want to turn into a Ted. I'm not just what I do. But who am I after retirement?

Part II: Chapter Three

(JOURNAL ENTRIES #3 & #4)

Journal Entry #3

It's not just the sad/happy state of being retired that bothers me. It's what's happening to me physically and mentally. I'm still working out at the gym, but when I look around at all those young hardbodies and then see myself in the mirror, I realize that I'm not like them anymore. Sure I'm pretty fit for my age—and that's part of the problem. Whenever someone comments on how I look or I take a critical glance at my physical condition, there is always that final tag line—for your age. As if I'm not supposed to be physically fit "at my age." What am I supposed to be? A deteriorating pile of skin and bones that needs to be helped with everyday tasks? I know I can't play basketball and tennis like I used to. Two artificial hips and an artificial right knee have seen to that. But there should be some honor to wearing out my joints from healthy, rugged physical activity. So I admit that I'm limited in my mobility and my speed. But does that make me less than those young people, or just different? I can out lift and out run a lot of men younger than me. Damn that tag line —"for his age"!

But I can't deny that I seem to get physically tired more easily than ever before. I go to bed earlier than I used to and I sleep longer than I used to. Maybe that's a reward for being loyal to my work and family responsibilities. Or is it because I can't now recuperate as fast as I once did? Does that mean there is something wrong with me? Because if it does, it doesn't make sense how well I feel each and every morning after a good night's sleep even though I go about waking up and meeting the day at a more leisurely pace.

But it's not just a question of physical conditioning. Although I hate to admit it, I feel some limitations to my physical well-being that have nothing to do with my conditioning. At my last check-up with my optometrist, I was told that I might be developing macular degeneration in both my eyes. That's an old person's condition! My hips and knee wore out, so now I'm a partial cyborg. I feel an ongoing stiffness in my muscles, something I only felt when I had the flu before. I have a bit of arthritis in my left thumb and in my right big toe. And I always sigh when I sit down.

Are these telltale signs that I'm wearing out? I can keep limber and strong by exercising and keeping active, but it's like my body is a rubber band—I can pull it into a kind of youthful liveliness, but it always snaps back after a while into a sense of slowing down and breaking down. For example, after I work out with the will and energy of my younger self, I feel exhilarated for a while, but then I hurt all over as if I had been hit by a truck. And perhaps I should not even bring up my pill regimen—for cholesterol, for blood pressure, for prevention of some kind of horrible infection in my hips and knee when I go to the dentist. So even though I try to eat well and keep moving, there is this sense that I'm staving off the inevitable. Seventy-three may be the new fifty-three, but it's nonetheless inching closer to ninety-three, and that's old! Don't our bodies have a built-in obsolescence like cars and computers? And what do you do with cars and computers that rust out and break down and become outmoded?

Journal Entry #4

I'm back at this journaling. Seems that it's become a habit for me.

I can write this journal entry with no problem right now, but I'm a bit anxious about whether I can keep on journaling. What I mean is, I'm also concerned about my mental health. I'm terrified at the prospect of developing some sort of dementia. I wonder whether that's one of the costs of getting older. I get a little worried because I'm more forgetful than ever. I experience "senior moments" when I can't follow my own train of thought. I sometimes wonder why I entered a room, sometimes I forget where I put my keys, sometimes I find myself repeating myself to keep my focus. Am I slipping? These kinds of mental lapses apparently are typical of "older adults," but are they a sign of mental deterioration? You're supposed to ward off dementia, especially Alzheimer's, by keeping mentally fit—doing crossword puzzles and sudokus, learning a new language, going back to school, having cognitively stimulating discussions, and I do all that. My question is whether all the prevention is effective.

Then there's something else. I immediately become offended when someone says something that even has the slightest implication that I'm not perfect. I am the teacher, not the student. I am an adult, not a child. I am the superior, not the inferior—no matter the circumstances, unless I choose to put myself in a subordinate state, like when I take classes at a local community college. Then I listen intently to the teacher. But that's because I have voluntarily placed myself in a lower position. I impulsively get angry and resentful when there is even a twinge of disrespect towards me, when I'm not treated as a person with authority who deserves deference. I believe I deserve respect because I have lived through so much and have learned so much and have figured out so much. Young people should come to me for wisdom, not demean me because I'm not as computer literate as they are or am not up on the latest fads or terminology.

I try hard to control this resentment and anger, but it springs up without warning. I've always been sensitive about my dignity, but this is irrationally compulsive. It helps me to understand how some "older" people act as if they deserve the last word on a topic or just expect to be treated as if that they were the experts on whatever topic is being discussed. It was so irritating when I was a young professional when an older person would make regal pronouncements about history as if they were always right. I was the actual student of history and I was a history teacher; they were just speaking off the top of their heads—and yet they demanded respect for their opinion. But now I'm doing the same thing, for God's sake! It's downright annoying! And there is something else.

When I'm criticized I sometimes snap back with a defense of myself, even when I know the criticism is well-deserved. And sometimes even when I defend myself, I take the criticism to heart so much that I begin a swirl of self-incrimination. I think: How could I have been so stupid? Shouldn't I have known better? Who am I to ever offer advice when I'm such a screw-up myself?

Where did all this come from? It wasn't my way of responding before.

If someone criticized me before, I was confident enough in myself to either dismiss the criticism or vigorously defend myself against it. But now sometimes when someone points out one of my bad habits or mistakes, even though I have successfully defended myself, I tend to rethink the criticism and take it very seriously. I double back on myself and recount how the criticism had some merit to it, then I get caught up thinking about all the stupid things I have ever done, all the mean things I have ever done, all the well-meaning mistakes I have ever made. Then I feel bad about myself and the negative impact I've made on the world. To keep me from falling down the rabbit hole of shame each time I am criticized or as a pre-emptive strike against criticism, I use self-deprecating humor. Then at least my listener will assure me that I am better than I judge myself to be.

So here I am with this question lodged right in my gut: Is my getting older the deterioration of all that made me me? Am I supposed to just accept the slow decline of my physical and mental and emotional powers? Is my deterioration inevitable? How am I supposed to live as I watch—no, live—my decline? Is there any value at all to getting older?

But I can't be the only one who has ever felt this way. Others must have questioned and fought this getting old crap. What would it be like to go back in time—become un-old? I can just imagine ...

Part II: Chapter Four

(DON'S STORY ABOUT BECOMING UN-OLD)

THE RING

The sun was high in the sky and its heat was oppressive. But Betty wanted to finish her gardening chores. She knew full well she should not have started this project as late in the day as she had, but there were other things that had to get done before she could clean up the flowerbed.

It was an unusually warm day, and even though she wore her wide-brimmed straw hat for protection, she still sweated profusely. The drops of sweat kept streaking her glasses, and she was annoyed at how often she had to wipe the lenses. She loved to be working in the earth and knew what she was doing was important. It was bringing beauty into the world, and it was clearing the way for the vegetables she would plant.

So even though she began to feel oppressed by the heat and needed to wipe the sweat from her brow more than she wanted to, Betty pressed on with her gardening shovel and rake. These flowers and plants were like her children. She cared for them and wanted them to prosper at the touch of her hand. Her real children had long ago grown up and moved away. But she still felt such joy taking care of something that could not take care of itself.

Gardening was not only productive; it was delightful. It made her feel needed and important. So she always put herself fully into weeding and digging around the plants and fertilizing them to keep them strong. She hoped that her hard work and persistence would result in beautiful flowers and delicious vegetables. And she hoped that her fingers would not swell so much that she would be uncomfortable all evening till she went to sleep.

That her legs would serve her well enough so that she could get up from her kneeling position without hanging on to the full-size rake handle which was just in reach. That her back would not stiffen up and ache so she would need a heating pad again.

Betty accepted the aches and pains her gardening brought on because she was proud of her work in the garden, just like she was proud of her many years as a beautician. She helped so many people to see their beauty and feel their worth because Betty was a skilled technician and a very good listener. Although she never went to college, never studied psychology or counseling, she had an intuitive sense of another person's state of mind and heart. She never gave advice, just helped her clients find answers in their own ways.

Betty knew she was no dummy. She understood how to help things to grow, to reach their potential in their own way, in their own time. She may have just passed her 83rd trip around the sun, but she was not just a vulnerable old lady.

Like that call she received a couple of days ago. The caller breathlessly told her that her grandson had been jailed in some foreign country and needed to receive $5,000 in bail money immediately—to be paid by credit card to an internet address in the United States. Sure, Betty had a grandson. Sure, he was old enough to travel to a foreign country. Sure, he was immature enough to get himself in trouble and need help getting out of a jam. But Betty's intuition told her to beware, and after acting as if she were concerned about the caller's request, she began asking questions that the caller had difficulty answering. So the caller abruptly hung up, and Betty's suspicions were confirmed. The call was nothing more than a scam directed at another elderly person who should have been an easy mark. Betty recognized that she was a senior, but she also believed her mind was as sharp as ever.

This thought brought a smile to Betty's face, and she began to sing out loud in the middle of the flowers and weeds. She didn't give a thought if anyone was listening. She liked feeling carefree and alive.

Then she came upon some stubborn weeds. So she began to dig them out and was surprised how deep their roots were. After a short while she had created quite a hole around the weeds, but finally she loosened them and tore them out of the ground. They were out. But the deep hole remained. So Betty turned to get some potting soil out of the bag nearby, but before she pivoted she was drawn to a bright, shiny object that stood out from the dirt around it. Intrigued, she put down her hand-shovel, took off her gardening gloves and raised the object up from its grave.

Betty brushed the dirt away and was surprised to see what appeared to be a silver metal ring like a wedding band. She held it up to get a good look at it and noticed that for all the time it had been buried it was in pristine shape. There were no scratches or dull patches. It was like it had recently been carefully polished.

She was intrigued, so she held it up to the sun and then brought it closer to carefully inspect it. *A silver ring,* she thought. *How odd, yet how interesting!* She rolled it around her fingers and then placed it in the palm of her right hand. She felt a slight warmth radiate from the ring, first to her palm and then out to her fingers. Then she picked it up with her left hand and tried putting it on the ring finger of her right hand (the left hand ring finger was reserved for her wedding ring which she continued to wear faithfully although her husband of 62 years had died four years ago). She would not be unfaithful to Hank if she were to wear this silver ring. After all, multiple rings were all the rage these days.

Betty tried on the ring, but she could not get it over her ring-finger knuckle which like her other knuckles had enlarged because of her arthritis. Then suddenly she felt a warmth radiating from the ring as she held it up. She thought she might just try again. And this time the ring fit over her boney knuckle as if it had willfully expanded to fit her finger. As she slipped it on she noticed with surprise that it seemed to contract to fit her finger perfectly. It was as if the ring attached itself to Betty. She held her hand out in front of her to admire how good the ring looked on her. It out-shown her wedding ring as if it were lit up by the sun.

"Now isn't this a lucky find," Betty said out loud. Then to protect the ring, she carefully covered it with her blue-flowered gardening glove and continued her work, thinking that no matter how trivial the results of her gardening were, finding the ring had made her efforts worthwhile. Betty really liked her new piece of jewelry. It made her feel like a queen.

Later, right before she laid down for the night, she slipped her wedding ring off and put it in a special case on her dresser. Then she tried to take off the silver ring. But no matter how hard she tried, it would not slip over her knuckle. It seemed as if the harder she tried to remove it, the more it clung to her finger. Eventually she gave up since it felt comfortable enough to continue to wear it. Then she laid down in her bed and quickly drifted off to sleep.

Betty woke up earlier than normal the next day but felt well-rested and full of energy. As was her usual routine, she walked from her bed directly into her bathroom. She turned the lights on so she could see herself in the mirror over the sink. And as she raised her head to look in the mirror, she was taken aback to see the crow's feet that usually appeared around her half-opened eyes were gone and the age spots that had dotted her face and arms had mysteriously disappeared. Most surprisingly, her breasts were no longer saggy. And she felt a warm sensation in them as if they had been revitalized.

Why would my two "girls" be feeling like this? she wondered. Then she recalled that they had felt this way years ago when she craved sexual encounter. *I'm well over that!* she thought. Then she wondered, and sure enough. She unbuttoned her pajama top and unlaced her pajama bottoms and stood before the mirror in only her panties. As she inspected herself in the mirror, she noticed that her breasts were firm and full and rounded and her "spare tire" had faded away.

"What's happening to me?" Betty asked the woman in the mirror, as if the image knew something she did not. She was so intrigued by this that she took off her panties and could not believe that her pubic hair had blackened, and the extra heft of her hips had retreated. Plus the cellulite that dimpled her thighs had gone away. She looked up and took a closer glimpse at the hair on her head. It was still grey, but it had definite black roots and seemed to have thickened considerably. "I'm getting younger!" she shouted. But she had no idea why or how this was happening. Still, she liked it. She was becoming un-old.

Betty left the bathroom and dressed for the day in clothes she had not worn for decades. She had missed that breezy, care-free fashion style she had adopted before she had even met Hank. Having children made dressing like that out of the question. She switched to being ever so practical, and never looked back, although she did keep her modish clothes back in the closet "just in case."

She bound down the stairs to her kitchen, made coffee and stepped onto her porch to retrieve the newspaper. As she reached down to pick it up, she noticed that she could bend down without feeling stiff and with no twinge of pain in her back. She twirled to go back in the house, and as she did, she began to hum. She threw the paper up in the air and caught it as if she were still the champion softball player she had been in high school.

The sun shone brightly, and the birds seemed to sing ever more sweetly. *This is truly the dawning of a new day for me*, Betty thought. And before she sat at the kitchen table to read the paper, she noticed her gardening hat placed on the clothes rack by the front door. *Not today*, Betty said to herself. *That's for an old lady.* But what to do with the day? Gardening was out. Reading books and watching TV were too boring for the way she felt. Then she spied an ad in the newspaper for a "spectacular sale" at Jonell's, a local fashion place. She had seen such ads for many years but had passed them over figuring they were not meant for her. But now she was enticed by the new styles. *A new me needs a new look*, she declared to herself. But she did not want to go shopping alone.

So Betty called a friend from her church choir at least thirty years her junior who had invited her on many occasions to go out with her on day-adventures as she called them. As Betty reached for the phone, she hesitated. *Is Claudette working? What would we have in common? Would she want to be seen with an old lady like me? But I don't look so much like an old lady now. I don't feel so much like an old lady now. It seems like a cloud has been lifted from my approach to my life. The last time I went to see the optometrist she said I was developing cataracts in both eyes. Well, maybe it wasn't cataracts in the eyes but a cataract over my attitude toward myself and my world. Maybe, just maybe, it will work out with Claudette.*

Betty dialed Claudette's number, and when Claudette answered, Betty sheepishly identified herself and asked if Claudette had some time today to go clothes shopping. Claudette responded enthusiastically that she had been waiting for Betty to take her up on her offer. She just happened to be off from work today and would love to spend the day with a lovely lady like Betty. So the deal was sealed. Claudette would pick Betty up around 11 am and they would spend the day shopping and eating and getting to know one another.

Betty put down the phone and hurried back upstairs to the bathroom to shower and groom for what promised to be a fun day. When she was finished, she dressed as stylishly as she could given that most of her clothes were purchased years ago and had not been worn for decades. But when Betty tried them on they fit perfectly, and with some creative thought, she accessorized them so well she could have been mistaken for a celebrity fashion plate.

Just before Claudette was due to pick her up, Betty looked one last time in the mirror. She was pleased to see that the grey had almost fully receded from her hairdo and the contour of her figure had returned to how it was prior to meeting Hank. She looked very much like a maiden rather than a matron.

When Claudette arrived, Betty walked jauntily to Claudette's car, opened the door and greeted her companion with, "Thank you for picking me up. It's so good to see you. I'm so looking forward to our having some fun today. Isn't it just a wonderful day!"

Claudette was surprised by Betty's vivacious start to their adventure. She looked at her with a questioning look but suppressed her desire to ask, "What's going on?" The woman who entered her car was not the same demur, soft-spoken, kindly elderly woman with her pancake makeup, rose water perfume and bluish tinted bouffant whom Claudette was drawn to.

"So nice to see you too, Betty. I was hoping we could get together, but it seemed like we could never connect. But here we are, free and daring." She hesitated and shot a glance at Betty who was looking at herself in her make-up mirror. "And I must say, aren't we indeed daring?" She was referring to the fact that Betty was wearing brightly colored clothes which included a skirt that came down no lower than the middle of her thighs. Claudette stifled her curiosity about Betty's attire and her overall look which belied her age. *83 isn't it? She looks like a woman in her 30's,* she thought to herself. The mystery had to wait till they could settle down and talk.

They arrived at the shopping mall, an expansive complex of stores, restaurants and night clubs. After Claudette parked, she and Betty headed straight for Jonell's at Betty's insistence. In the store Betty was like a tornado, whipping through the dresses and tops and pants and accessories. She picked out a blinding array of new clothes and then tried them on with the long-suffering Claudette acting as her fashion critic. Because Betty so liked one outfit, she paid for it and wore it out of the store, having the clerk box up the clothes she brought from home.

Betty was enjoying her shopping spree, but Claudette was exhausted by it. So she suggested to Betty that they take a break from their fashion tsunami with some lunch. Although Betty wanted to continue with boundless energy, she gave in to her friend's entreaties with the hope that if she gave in to Claudette's suggestions now, then Claudette would be obliged to give in to hers later.

The two of them left Jonell's, Betty with multiple bags of clothes on both arms. Claudette had none. They settled on a trendy small restaurant that promised good food and good drink. They were given a food menu and a drink menu, and as soon as the waiter came to their table, Betty ordered a cocktail. Claudette ordered white wine. Both women then made a beeline to the restroom to freshen up.

While in front of the large mirror that spanned the south wall of the entire bathroom, Betty noticed more changes in her appearance. Her hair was as dark as it was when she was thirty and her breasts were downright perky! Gone were all her face lines. Her shoulders were no longer stooped and her waist rivaled Scarlett O'Hara's. When Claudia emerged from the stall, she remarked that Betty seemed to be getting younger by the minute. Betty beamed at this remark.

When the two returned to their table, their drinks were waiting for them. Claudette proposed a toast to friendship and freedom. Betty lifted her glass to Claudette and laughed a hearty laugh.

"What's so funny?" Claudette asked.

"I feel so free that I can't hold it inside anymore."

"Is it because of how you look?"

"It's because I look young and I feel young. The energy and power of my youth have returned. I'm a new woman, Claudette."

"I can see that," replied Claudette tongue in cheek. "What have you been doing to yourself? A new diet? A magical exercise regimen? A young and handsome personal trainer?"

"None of those. It all happened incredibly overnight."

"I think that drink has gone to your head, my friend."

"No, it's true. I woke up this morning and noticed that my transformation had begun, and when I was in the bathroom just now, I noticed that it was continuing. I am definitely getting younger as we speak."

"But how can that be? Has something happened to you? Is there anything that's changed in your life?"

"Not really, except for this." And Betty showed Claudette the silver ring that was shining brighter than ever.

"I found this buried in my garden yesterday. I put it on, and it won't come off. It's like it has wedded itself to my finger. And now I'm different. But it's good, good, as you can see." And Betty stuck out her chest and patted her raven black shiny hair.

"Are you sure this is a good thing?"

"Of course it is. I feel great. No more elder aches and pains. No more constant fatigue. No more thinking about dying. All I think about now is living, living, living!"

"Seriously, what would Hank think about all this?"

"Hank who?"

"Your husband who you were married to for 62 years. And what about your children?"

Betty looked confused. "Husband? Children? I'm footloose and fancy free. Got my whole life ahead of me. I think I might go to school to become a real estate agent."

"What about being a beautician? You've got a great reputation from your work there."

"I don't know what you're talking about." And with this remark Claudette began to worry.

Just then the waiter brought Betty another cocktail, one she had not ordered. And when she asked why he had given it to her, he pointed to a strapping young man sitting alone at a table not too far from where the two friends were sitting. "It's from him," said the waiter who walked away.

Betty looked at her benefactor and immediately began to flirt with him. From that moment, she was so sorely distracted that she rudely ignored the woman sitting across from her.

Claudette was quite aware of what was happening, and she became angry and offended when in the middle of their conversation Betty walked over to the man with her drink in hand. When Betty returned to the table, she noticed that Claudette was gathering her things as if she were ready to leave.

Claudette spat out, "Here's the money for my wine. Why don't you get your friend to drive you home?"

"No problem," replied Betty, "He's already offered to do that."

Then Claudette turned and left in a huff, and the man casually walked over to where Claudette had been sitting and asked, "Is this seat taken?"

Betty laughed coyly and motioned for him to sit down. It was clear that she wanted a connection with this young stud. He was dark-skinned with jet black hair. He was wearing a blue and red flashy silk shirt with tight leather pants that accentuated his crotch. Betty was aroused, and she wanted nothing more than to have his arms around her. Clearly he wanted the same, and as they talked and ordered more drinks, they both became more and more vulnerable to their desires. So they decided not to eat but to go somewhere nearby where they could connect more intimately than they could in public.

They walked out of the restaurant arm-in-arm laughing at silly little jokes that prepared them for the seriousness of the situation they were facing. The young man suggested that they walk just a couple blocks where he had his bachelor pad. There were more drinks available there and he had some very romantic music he wanted to share.

Betty let herself be swept up in the moment. She felt pushed along by the longing in her breasts and the sweetness she felt in her groin. There was no recollection of being this way before. It was like a first-time experience. She had no clue how to play this situation, so she let herself float on the flow of the desire.

When they arrived at the apartment which was well-appointed in the style of a person of supreme self-confidence and urbane taste, the young man invited Betty to have a seat on a brown leather couch while he prepared drinks for them both and put on some "lovely" music. Betty fidgeted a bit but was determined to go through with what she so ached to do.

The young man put on romantic music featuring a slow wailing saxophone. He came into the room where Betty was waiting nervously and handed her a strong cocktail. "To us," he said as he raised his glass to Betty. He encouraged her to empty her glass quickly, which she did. It reached her stomach with a warmth that seemed to dispel her fears. The young man took the empty glass from her and put it on the black glass coffee table in front of the couch. Then he moved over to where she was sitting and gently took her hand. His touch seemed electric and Betty yielded to her urge to let him touch more than her hand. So he did. He kissed her softly on her forehead, then on her cheeks, then full on her mouth. Her lips molded to his, and soon their tongues touched and pressed against each other. His hands at first gently touched her face, then they migrated to her neck, then they dropped to her breasts and gently cupped them. Betty put her head back and let out a soft sigh, which the young man took as permission to unbutton her blouse and pull down her bra. He gently kissed her full pink breasts and gently squeezed her hard and erect nipples till Betty began to shudder with pleasure.

Then Betty fantasized about what was coming next, but she hesitated to give in to his advances because she knew she was not yet ready for that. So she gently pushed him away and gathered her blouse about her. "I need to use the bathroom first, Lover. I'll be just a moment." The man tried to stop her, but when she insisted, he pulled back frustrated and resentful all at once.

Betty hurried into the bathroom that was decorated with golden fixtures and a full-length mirror lighted by bright bulbs fashioned for professional makeup duties. Betty looked at her reflection and was embarrassed by what he saw. A vague memory awakened in her of making love with Hank. Then she reached deep down in her soul and found a disgust for where she was headed now. The ring may have taken away the signs of physical aging and wiped away the wisdom she had gathered from 83 years of life experience, but it had not disconnected her completely from a sense of her own dignity and what she thought was important.

As she looked at herself in the mirror, Betty said to herself, *I like this new me. It's exciting and filled with fresh experiences. But it also makes me start all over again. Look at me! Is this what I really am? Am I a slut? I may be losing myself to this new body and mind, but I am the same soul and spirit I always was.*

And with this deep sense that she would be disgraced and shamed by giving in to the lust that still lingered within her, Betty adjusted her bra and blouse and dashed out of the bathroom like a woman on a mission. When she came upon the young man who had his arms out inviting her to continue where they left off, she spit out, "No thank you. I'm not like that!" Then she angrily picked up her purse and the shopping bags which were laid near the door to the apartment, opened the door and ran out of the apartment without looking back.

As she ran back to the shopping mall, she thought, *I must get home where I belong.* So Betty hailed a cab that was luckily just then coming toward her, got in and gave the driver her home address. And as she was driven to her house, she felt guilt and sadness about how she had treated Claudette who only wanted to spend a day of friendship and fun with her. She began to cry bitterly, and the taxi driver overheard her. He looked in his rear-view mirror at the pathetic sight he was transporting and asked if everything was all right.

"Yes, yes. I'm all right. I just had a shameful and embarrassing experience that I wish had never happened. And I hope will never happen again, if there is anything I have to say about it." And Betty meant that.

So the ride which had taken only about ten minutes seemed to have taken ten hours because Betty was terribly anxious to get out of the car, run to her house and return to her real self. When they arrived and the taxi driver parked in front of Betty's house, she paid him the fare along with a generous tip, dropped her packages on the sidewalk and ran headlong to her garden. *At least I remember where I live and where the garden is,* she thought.

When she reached the garden, Betty focused on the place where she had found the silver ring. She sprinted to the very spot where she had come upon it and tried to take it off. But it would not budge. It did not fit over her knuckle. She tried and tried, desperately attempting to detach it and cancel its power. But every time she struggled to drag it up and over her knuckle, it snapped back to where it was as if it had rooted itself into her finger.

Betty panicked. She looked around the area for something she could use to free herself from the ring's grasp. Then she spied a small hatchet partially covered with garden soil and rust. She had long forgotten that it was there.

How does it go? she said to herself. *If your hand leads to evil, cut it off? Better to get into heaven with only one hand than to fall into hell with two.* It didn't matter that she could not get the quote exactly right. She knew what it meant. So Betty picked up the hatchet and walked over to the large rock that guarded a corner of her backyard.

She placed the blade of the hatchet at the base of her finger to set her aim and raised the hatchet above her head to power it to its target. But as she held the hatchet up with every intention to rid herself of this evil spirit, her knuckle receded in size and the ring slipped off her hand on its own. It fell to ground by the edge of the boulder into some neglected weeds. When it touched the soil, it burrowed itself into the dirt till it disappeared.

Relieved and thankful, Betty put the hatchet down and began to feel violently ill, so she sat on the rock. But matters got worse and she pitched headfirst to the ground and convulsed. She shook, she sweated, she felt paralyzed. Then it was over, and as she sat back down on the rock, she noticed that her new clothes were torn, and she had returned to her previous matronly figure. The age spots were back, the worry lines had returned, and her breasts resumed their droop.

Betty was tired, so very tired, but she was happy. She knew she would have to make up with Claudette for what she had put her through, but otherwise, she was back. And it was good to be back. She had lost herself because she was not satisfied with herself.

Betty stood up, returned to the front of her house, gathered her packages and went inside. It was good to be home. It was good to know that the faded picture on her fireplace was of the handsome man she had married. And the toys scattered about the house were from her grandchildren who filled the house with their laughter and liveliness. These things were not new, but now they were fresh to her. And she appreciated them like never before.

Since the sun was still out although evening was upon her, Betty changed her clothes, put on her large-brimmed straw hat, picked up her garden tools and kneeler from the garage and walked out into the sun to her garden. *This is where I belong*, she felt. *I don't have to go through it all over again. I have more to offer than what I had when I was my younger me. Nothing is going to take all that away from me ever again. I like my later self. It's colored with the joys and scars and wisdom that come with all my many years.*

Here I am. I am more than before. I have more to give. And my petunias and peas need me. I know just what to do. Then she knelt down, grabbed her hand hoe and began to loosen the dirt around her flowers. And her smile rivaled the sun with its radiance.

Being younger ain't all it's cracked up to be! Maybe I should be content with getting older. But what does "getting older" really mean?

Part II: Chapter Five

(JOURNAL ENTRIES #5 & #6)

Journal Entry #5

I just came back from a funeral. I hate funerals. They're such gloomy and sad affairs. And that's not like Tim was. He was a great guy. Always happy. Always joking. He was 70. As far as I'm concerned, he was a young man. Died in the flower of his age. Heart attack. Not that it wasn't expected. He didn't really take good care of himself. Drank, smoked, did whatever he wanted. He joked that if he was going to go, he was going to go happy. He always said, "Why worry about how you live? It's all in the cards anyway. How does it go: Eat, drink and be merry for tomorrow we die?"

But I'm not so sure we have nothing to say about our death. Seems to me we can bring it about or hold it off by some simple lifestyle choices. I know I will die. But I hate when someone tells me that since I'm 73 I'm closer to death than they are. Who knows that to be true? Could slip on ice and crack your head. Could get in some freak accident. Could throw some type of blood clot and freeze your brain. So I'm not so sure I'm closer to death than someone younger than me, but I know I'm closer to death than I was at 35. It seems to me the question of my death is not about looking back at my life; it's about looking to the future. And frankly, sometimes I get scared when I think about "end-of-life issues."

I must admit I do get concerned over my death sometimes. I guess for a lot of reasons. When will it happen? How will it happen? Why does it have to happen? Why can't I just go on and on? And what's on the other side of death? Anything?

If there's nothing after death, then what's my life really been all about? Why wouldn't I have done all the things I've wanted to do but didn't because I thought they would get me in trouble later on? Why have I not just hooked myself up to a narcotic drip and hallucinated till my body calls it quits? What am I talking about?! That seems like running away from life rather than living it. I don't want to be reduced to something like that! Especially since I have experienced many good and wonderful things in my life that have made my life worth living. And every one of those things implied that death is not life's conclusion even though it may be life's final act.

This journaling has made me think about some important things. That's for sure. But am I closer to any answers? I'm getting older, moving closer to my death. Should I prepare for it or just let it happen?

That's enough for now. My head is beginning to hurt.

Journal Entry #6

I read over my entry on death from the other day. Brings up lots of things to think about. But it does not satisfy my concerns about death and growing old. Prime among all these concerns is this one: Why do we age at all? Why can't we just stay young and never die?

It seems that every living thing goes through the same stages of life—goes from seed to sprout to maturity to deterioration to death. Apparently I can delay the more painful and limiting aspects of this process, but I can't stop it. Life always ends in death. But why? Some people live into their 100's, but have you seen them? They're all wrinkled and crinkled. Even people who take good care of themselves seem to end that way. Is this a sign that going away from this world is built into every living thing? Is my life a procession to my death? If so, why live to begin with? Why endure the pains and challenges that come with life if life always ends in a whimper? Is it all worth it?

Surely I'm closer to my death than I have ever been before. Maybe I should find out what death means. Should I look forward to death or go into it kicking and screaming? Should I just shrug my shoulders with a "so what" attitude? Should my death matter to me? The death of others matters to me, but my death is different. My death can't matter to me when I'm already dead, so it's got to be that my death should matter to me before it happens.

But all this thinking about death is depressing. Shouldn't I just dismiss death from my mind and my heart and go on living as if I will go on living? But living for what?

Maybe death works like a deadline that motivates us to seek out and take up opportunities before it's too late. If my life went on and on, I probably would have a procrastinator's attitude toward it. Here in the Midwest, farmers must plant at a certain time of the year, so their crops can grow during a different time of the year, so that they can be gathered at another time of the year. Farmers cannot be successful if they do their farming haphazardly without considering what they are planting, where they are planting it and what kind of weather they can expect.

Seems the same goes for my life. To live well I need to consider the fact that I will die, and I need to consider what that means. In a sense I am like a seed planted in this world. My actions are the care I give to my growth and well-being. Then there is death. So is death the reaping of what I have done and become, or is it just a "dying on the vine" and senseless? It all depends on what death is. Is it a wall or a door? Do I go crashing into it and come apart never to be put together again? Or do I get the chance to open it to a new way of being me, a way that I should be preparing for all my life? Is my death a "too bad" or a "farewell"?

But I can't be the only one who has ever felt this way. Others must have thought long and hard about death and how to approach it. What would dying be like if it was very much up to me? I can just imagine …

59

Part II: Chapter Six

(DON'S STORY ABOUT DEALING WITH DEATH)

LEAVING

It was a little past noon when Fr. Joseph Randell walked into his home on the grounds of the church he served, slumped into his favorite easy chair and poured himself a short glass of scotch. It was too early in the day to be drinking, he knew, but he really needed a drink right then.

Fr. Joe had just officiated at a funeral of a promising high school athlete who had been run over by a drunk driver. He had led the congregation in prayers and reflections that were meant to console the boy's devastated family as were the white cloth draped over the casket, the songs of hope from the choir, and the Scripture readings that spoke of being enfolded in the loving arms of God and brought home. But no matter the hope and solace offered by the ceremony, the family were beside themselves with deep, searing sorrow. And Fr. Joe's heart went out to them. He hurt too, and that was the problem. It took so much emotional energy to recover from such shared anguish that Fr. Joe just had to be alone for a while. Normally when he found himself in this state, he read Scripture and just sat silently to be in tune with the love of God. But today was different. This was the third funeral this week, and there had been two funerals last week. How much pain and grief and confusion he had witnessed and shared in! There was no time now for prayer and silence. He needed immediate relief from the dark feelings that had overcome him.

What made matters worse was that even though Fr. Joe shared in their agony, he could not let anyone know what he was feeling. Because he had to be strong for them. Because he had to bring what he believed to be the very real message of God's love for them despite what had happened and how they were feeling. So he repressed his dark, foreboding feelings. And he could do this rather well when there were only random instances of pain and sorrow, but this recent combination of sad and draining events had been too much. And what made it worse was that he was basically alone. Sure he had some priest friends and some parishioners who regularly invited him to their houses for dinner and conversation. Sure there was always the parish youth group that buoyed his spirit with endless energy and promise. And sure, he knew full well that God was always near. But at moments like these he could not help but crave the comfort of another human being.

As he sat there, Fr. Joe began to fantasize about going out on a date with a beautiful woman. But he caught himself because he knew that if he took this fantasy too far it would simply lead to frustration and a deeper longing for what his position would not allow. To avoid temptation he quickly rose from his chair and made himself a bowl of tomato soup and a BLT sandwich, his favorite lunch combo. Now he believed he would be ready for the rest of the day.

Two weeks went by with surprisingly little for Fr. Joe to do other than his routine parish work. He visited the sick, presided over daily Mass and performed all the menial administrative tasks his pastoral position entailed. However, he did look forward to the parish high school youth group's monthly meeting happening in two days. He really enjoyed being with the kids. Fr. Joe delighted in their lust for life and hope for their future. He had a rapport with them that assured them he was their friend as well as their spiritual mentor. Occasionally he would counsel some of the youths who had personal problems, but the sessions would be random and short. He hoped he had done some good. But Fr. Joe was unaware of what lurked for him with this meeting.

The youth group always met in the parish gym because the members would rather sit on the floor than in chairs like at school. When Fr. Joe entered the room, the young people greeted him in unison, which brought a big smile to his face. Some of the young men went up to him and shook his hand, and some of the young women went up to him and hugged him.

Fr. Joe allowed this because he felt it established the kind of open and kind accessibility that this demographic wanted and needed.

Last in the line to hug the priest was Leslie Cortrell, a pretty blond-haired girl who was a junior at the high school and a prominent member of the cheerleading squad. She was Fr. Joe's height, athletically built and buxom, especially for her age. She threw herself at Fr. Joe with an enthusiasm that far outstripped how the other girls had approached the priest. She hugged him tightly and whispered in his ear, "I love you so much!" Although Fr. Joe felt uncomfortable with this kind of hug and the words of greeting, he tried not to show his displeasure and fear so he would not detract from the jovial atmosphere in the gym. He gently pulled away from Leslie and said in a matter-of-fact way, "Love ya too, kid." Leslie scowled. *She certainly was no kid!* Feeling rebuffed, she returned to her group of friends.

The meeting started with a prayer led by Fr. Joe. Then the youth leaders talked about upcoming events, led the group in lively faith-based songs, and served pizza and soft drinks. Fr. Joe, roman collar and all, sat cross-legged on the gym floor with all the others. Laughter filled the area and everyone seemed to be in a good mood. That is, everyone but Leslie who had retreated to a corner of the room surrounded by some of her girlfriends. Fr. Joe noticed this and broke himself away from the round of jokes that were being passed around with the rest of the youth group, wiped his face and stepped up to the little crowd formed around Leslie.

"Is anything wrong?" asked Fr. Joe with a look of kindly concern. Suzie Brockton, Leslie's best friend, took the priest aside and explained that Leslie was very upset because she had just learned that her parents were getting a divorce because her father had been having a secret affair. Fr. Joe thanked Suzie for the information and turned back to where Leslie was tearfully sitting on a folding chair in the middle of the group. Barbara Samson, a fellow cheerleader, was kneeling beside Leslie with her arm draped gently around the weeping girl's shoulders.

Fr. Joe came up to Leslie and knelt next to Barbara. "What's wrong, Leslie?" he asked softly with all the compassion he could muster.

Leslie looked at him with tears streaking her eyeliner. "I can't tell you here, Father. Would you come with me into the equipment room so we can talk in private?"

"I think I can arrange that," Fr. Joe responded naively.

Fr. Joe first looked at Barbara who nodded that she understood. Then when he stood up, she motioned for all the others to go back to the rest of the group. They did so, and Fr. Joe was left alone with Leslie. He gently helped her up and offered her his clean handkerchief while taking from her the tattered napkin that she was using to dry her tears. Then they left the gym and walked next door to the equipment room where the pizzas and drinks had been stored.

There were two folding chairs in the room, so Fr. Joe set one up for Leslie and opened the other one for himself. He sat across from her with his hands folded in his lap. She looked up at him with black mascara staining her rosy cheeks and said, "Father, I'm so upset. I don't know what to do. I just found out that my parents are divorcing because of my dad's being unfaithful. Why would he do such a thing, Father?" Her sorrow now mixed with anger. "My mother's a wonderful person. Of course she's not some high-and-mighty lawyer like my dad, but she's always been a loving and decent wife and certainly the best mom to me and Tommy ever. I hope he rots in hell!"

"Now, Leslie, it'll be all right," Fr. Joe counseled. "The Lord will take care of you and your mother and brother. He will deal with your father as He sees fit. Our God is a God of mercy, but He is also a God of justice, and it's up to God to deal with your dad's misdeeds, not you. I know that you're hurting pretty bad now. Can't blame you at all. If there is anything I can do to help you and your family through this crisis, please let me know."

Leslie's gaze at Fr. Joe expressed more than appreciation for his sympathetic words. She wiped her eyes and said, "Father, could you hold me? I really need that right now."

Fr. Joe sat silent and confused for a minute. He knew he had the power to heal as a minister of God and he knew that he felt Leslie's pain. Yet he hesitated to respond because here before him sat a very vulnerable under-aged young lady whom he wanted to hold, but he knew that to do so might be mis-understood. Or even more frightening, might be understood for what beneath his kind words and gestures of sympathy it really was—his own escape from loneliness. Fr. Joe was torn between his role as a spiritual guide and healer and his deep need for intimacy.

Before he could decide how to answer this dilemma, Leslie rose, reached out her arms to him, took hold of his hands and pulled him out of his chair and close to her. She wrapped herself around him like she wanted to melt completely into him. Fr. Joe found himself reaching around her athletic yet soft body until his hands met in the middle of her back. Then Leslie pulled back a little and kissed him squarely on his lips, a gesture that sent shudders throughout the priest's body. And without thinking his hands slipped from the middle of the young lady's back to her rounded muscular rump. His fingers began to tingle at the touch, and Leslie's body seemed to arch toward him as if she wanted to be even closer.

Leslie slowly moved forward to kiss the priest again, but instead of lending himself to the gesture, he became startled and afraid. *What am I doing?* he asked himself. *I may be a man, but I'm also a priest. This is not what I'm supposed to do. She has come to me for support, and what have I given her? A passport to sex? Father, forgive me for what I have done!*

Fr. Joe abruptly yanked himself from Leslie's arms and held her at arms-length saying, "This is not why we have come here, Young Lady. I know it and you know it. You know I am here for you as your pastor and friend, nothing more. And if that's not enough, I'm sorry, really I am."

Leslie was no longer crying because she was angry. Angry that she had been rebuffed, angry that he had called her a "young lady," angry that her family and now the one person she thought could give her what she needed at this most difficult time in her life had let her down. She spun around away from Fr. Joe and stepped in front of a full-length mirror so that there would be no evidence of what had happened. She put on her cheerleader face and bolted out of the equipment room and returned to the party in the gym where music was playing and her friends were dancing.

Fr. Joe stood transfixed to his spot. What was he going to do now? But he could not ponder that. He had to go back into that gym and act as if he had been faithful to his roles of pastor and friend.

Matters raced forward from that moment, and they went from bad to worse. Leslie told her parents about what had happened in that equipment room hoping they would somehow get back together now that they had a common enemy. That plan did not work out because her father blamed her mother for putting Leslie in such a vulnerable situation with her "churchy" approach to her upbringing. The incident drove them even further apart, but the incident had more far-reaching consequences than making a domestic matter even worse.

Leslie used the incident, not just to try to reunite her parents, but to enhance her reputation with her girlfriends at school. She hinted at what might have happened between Fr. Joe and her in that private moment so that the high school gossip mill eventually blew the incident into a full-blown sexual escapade between another Catholic priest and another underage, vulnerable young person.

Leslie's friends at school could not keep this juicy secret to themselves so they spread it about along with any tantalizing bits of speculation they could come up with. This eventually reached the ears of some of the parents of Leslie's friends who became outraged and bent on taking action against another predator priest.

One parent from Fr. Joe's parish even wrote a scathing letter to the bishop decrying such behavior, especially considering the scandal that was plaguing the church at the time. And the bishop had no choice but to suspend Fr. Joe from his pastoral duties due to the allegation as was mandated by church policy meant to protect "God's children" from inappropriate behavior. A church and a civil inquiry ensued, which both found their way into the local newspaper. The bishop eventually "suggested" that Fr. Joe relocate while the investigations were ongoing, and Fr. Joe knew that he needed to leave so he would not further undermine the parishioners' trust in their parish. So Fr. Joe moved to his uncle and aunt's house in the Cleveland, Ohio suburbs.

On the day Fr. Joe crossed over the threshold of Uncle Fred and Aunt Lilly's two-story house, he could not help but think about how much lonelier he was now than he was back at the rectory. *I am a pariah. Now I know how Romeo felt when he was banished from Verona. My uncle and aunt are good, loving people, and I know they will support me no matter what I am accused of doing or really did. But I feel so isolated. Like Dante said, hell is ice, not fire. It is being torn away from everyone and everything else, and most of all from God who is the source and end of life. I have given all I could to His purposes. But I am a man, not an angel. I have needs and flaws. Am I to be condemned and disposed of for a natural inclination? I was tempted but did not give in. Why be punished for that? She led me on. But she is a child; I am an adult. It looks like something it's not, but it's not nothing either. Now it's possible that I will*

*never work with a faith community ever again. Never to work with the young
believers who are the promise of the future for the church and the world at large!
It is just too much to bear right now. I am without words or feelings. How kind
my relatives are, especially since my parents are dead and my sister out of state.
She is to never know!*

Fr. Joe hugged both Fred and Lilly but said little as he entered the
house with his luggage in hand. "Thank you for taking me in, Uncle Fred
and Aunt Lilly. You are very kind," is all he said. His hosts knew he was
hurting so they silently showed him to his upstairs room, and as they left
the room Aunt Lilly casually mentioned that they would be eating in about
half an hour. They said little else. What could they say at a time like this?

The investigations continued, an "administrator" was assigned to take
care of the parish in Fr. Joe's absence, and Fr. Joe prayed about and pondered
his fate. Sometimes he felt panic; sometimes he felt victimized; always he
felt sad and regretful. He tried his best to be good company to his aunt and
uncle, but they could tell he was forcing himself to be congenial. They were
sad for him. They did not know the particulars of his situation, but they
knew their Joey was hurting. And just to be sure nothing bad would happen
to him, they routinely checked on him in whatever room he happened to
be, drove him wherever he wanted to go and accompanied him whenever he
walked away from the house.

Two months passed and Fr. Joe seemed to be getting better. His mood
lifted and his appetite returned. Fred and Lilly were no longer afraid of
leaving him alone. So they no longer accompanied him on his frequent
walks to the nearby woods. They let him drive their car for short distances.
They even asked him to do some shopping for household items. They
refused to take any remuneration for their hospitality. Then it happened.

About three months into his stay in the morning when the day was
bright and the sky clear, Fr. Joe asked if he could use his aunt and uncle's
older car. Since they had two cars in the garage and Joey had asked to use
the older and less reliable of the two, they saw no reason to deny him access
to it, although they did wonder why he specified using the older of the two
cars. When they asked where he was going, he nonchalantly answered that

he needed to run some errands and might even take in a movie. This looked like a good sign to Fred and Lilly, so they handed Fr. Joe the keys and said, "God be with you, Sweetheart," as he left.

Fr. Joe drove directly to the commuter train station. He parked the car in the train depot parking lot with a letter in it for his aunt and uncle and anyone else who would want to know what he was planning to do. He began to cry as he left the letter on the dashboard, but he steeled himself for what he knew he had to do. He bought a ticket to downtown Cleveland and boarded the train in the early afternoon.

On the way to Cleveland, Fr. Joe spied a newspaper that had been left on a seat. He picked it up and started to read it. Only the middle section was there, and it contained the obituaries. He began to read the blurbs that were written below the flattering pictures of the deceased.

What will people say at my funeral? he thought to himself. *I have said so many kind and comforting words about other people at the funeral Masses I presided at. Will the priest have the same kind and comforting words to remember me? Will anyone be there? Will there even be a Mass for me?* And his mind raced and swirled with thoughts about what happened, about what life is all about, what death is all about, what would be in store for him when he dies. Eventually all this thinking and emotional stress led to Fr. Joe's exhaustion. And he fell asleep lulled by the slight rocking of the passenger car on the tracks.

Fr. Joe arrived at the old, stately hotel about 3:30 pm and went directly to the front desk. He asked for a single room on the top floor. The desk clerk told him that there was only one room left on that floor. It was in the back of the hotel overlooking an empty concrete lot, not a very good view. Fr. Joe said that he was unconcerned about the view and pre-paid the bill for an overnight stay. When the clerk asked if he needed any help with his luggage, Fr. Joe showed him his overnight bag and explained that this was all the luggage he had.

Fr. Joe stepped into the elevator and got off on the 10th floor. Being one of the oldest hotels in the city, the building needed remodeling. Its décor was clearly from the early 1900's. Fr. Joe dismissed this because he was intent upon his mission. He came to his room, unlocked the door with a metal key and entered the room to be greeted by something out of the 1920's. It didn't matter how the room appeared because he did not plan to remain in it for very long.

He threw his bag on the floor and sat down on the bed. The bed creaked with his weight. He was glad he did not have to sleep on it that night. Then Fr. Joe took off his jacket, walked into the bathroom and washed his hands and face. He felt anxious yet relieved that it soon would be all over. And maybe some good would come of it. He had left the letter in the car explaining what he was doing and why, and he had a copy in his bag that he would leave on the bed. Then he got himself ready.

Fr. Joe placed his overnight bag on the bed and removed a black clerical shirt. He put it on along with his Roman collar. He was going to be a priest to the end, no matter what anyone said. Then he removed two golden candle sticks, stuck unused white candles in them and placed them on the writing desk that was in the corner of the room. He made sure not to light them because he did not want anyone else to be hurt.

From his night bag Fr. Joe then took out a piece of paper on which he had printed some bible verses. He carefully placed the paper between the candles, then he took out a pyx from the bag and placed it on the paper. The pyx contained a consecrated host; the paper contained these three verses:

"What terrible things will come on the world through scandal! It is inevitable that scandal should occur. Nonetheless, woe to that man through whom scandal comes!" (Matt 18:7) Next to these words he had written in longhand, "Through me! But I never meant to, and I tried not to."

Underneath these words was written: "For I am certain that neither death nor life, neither angels nor principalities, neither the present nor the future, nor powers, neither height nor depth nor any other creature, will be able to separate us from the love of God that comes to us in Christ Jesus, our Lord." (Rom 8:38-39) Next to these words he had scribbled, "I know that God will <u>always</u> be with me and in me, no matter what."

Finally the paper read: "You spread the table before me in the sight of my foes; You anoint my head with oil; my cup overflows. Only goodness and kindness follow me all the days of my life; and I shall dwell in the house of the Lord for years to come." (Psalm 23:5-6) There were no words after this verse, only what looked like a dried teardrop. Fr. Joe smiled knowingly as he read these words out loud in prayer. Here was his solace. He had gone through his Gethsemane moment back at his aunt and uncle's house, all alone, quietly, in secret. But now he was ready to do what he believed he was called to do—to end it, to make it good, to fulfill the promise of his priesthood.

After reciting the Scripture verses, Fr. Joe prayed the "Our Father" then took out the host from the pyx. He said, "I am not worthy that You should enter under my roof. Say but the word, and my soul shall be healed." He then made the sign of the cross with the host, softly said, "Joey, body of Christ," and with great reverence placed the host on his tongue.

He made no sound except to whimper as he sat motionless on the bed with his head down and his hands folded on his lap. Then it was time.

Fr. Joe, the priest who trusted that he was chosen by God to lead believers and to convert unbelievers, the man who tried so hard to be faithful to his clerical vows, the sinner who lapsed just enough to bring about the crumbling of his life, stood up from the bed and walked to the window calmly with the resignation that comes from a firm decision. The window was encased in an old-style frame, and although it was sealed shut, it yielded to the Swiss Army knife Fr. Joe kept in his pocket for just such challenges. He forced the window open, which was not an easy task since it was old and had been shut for many years. Then he stuck his head outside the open window, and as he had hoped, there was a slight ledge beneath it. It was just wide enough for a full-grown man to stand on. He climbed out of the window without looking down and stood very still, pressing his body hard against the building.

Fr. Joe's heart was pounding, and his head was spinning. Should he go through with it or not? What did his soul tell him to do? He knew he could not take back what had happened, and he could not make matters better. If he stayed alive the pain to him and to so many others would just go on and on, and he simply could not let that happen. That's not what a person dedicated to God and to the love of all people would do.

He thought about the three Scripture quotes and he thought about death. He knew he was with the Lord, he knew that God was a God of mercy, he knew that NOTHING could separate him from the Jesus he had embraced ever since he was a child making his first communion. He was convinced that what he was about to do would be in the name of that Jesus, and like that Jesus he would be giving his life for many—and he would be throwing himself into the arms of God as he threw himself from the building.

Then Fr. Joe took a deep breath, closed his eyes and stretched out his arms to form a cross. He leaned forward and was released from the grasp of the ledge. Like a cliff diver he fell forward with his arms spread wide and his lips repeating, "Jesus, Jesus, Jesus," till he hit the concrete in the empty lot headfirst. There he laid crushed and bloody and lifeless. And a church bell began to ring in the distance. For whom did the bell toll? It tolled for Fr. Joe.

What a tragic end for Fr. Joe! Dying by his own hands. How will my end be? I'm going to die, and it seems that how I die depends a lot on how I live. How should I live now that I'm older and closer than ever to my own death?

Part II: Chapter Seven

(JOURNAL ENTRIES #7 & #8)

Journal Entry #7

I visited a nursing home today. I've visited there before as part of a church ministry, and I've always come back home feeling good because of how I could care for the sick and infirm who lived there. But this time it was different. I kept thinking of myself as someone who was stuck there. It was clean enough and comfortable enough, but it was filled with old people. I don't particularly like being surrounded by old people. They make me feel old. No, better yet, all those old people make me feel aged, outmoded, decrepit. And today I realized that I could just as well be one of them. I'm advanced in years, but I don't feel old. Yet I can't help but fear that someday I will end up there, dependent and weak. I really hate when some of the residents feebly call out for someone to take them home. Even now that breaks my heart. But their sons and daughters are not monsters. Maybe they really think this is the best way to take care of them. After all, aren't the younger members of the family paying for the care of their elderly? But who among the elderly want to be taken care of? They were once the caretakers, the bread winners, the achievers who saw their lives full of promise because they were strong and wise. But these poor people are either on the edge of losing their strength and wisdom or have already lost what made them them. The memory care unit is just exhaustingly sad.

Even though I don't feel older, all I have do to is look at pictures of me in my younger days. I'm still me but a different way of being me. My hair is grey and thinning, lines streak my face, the skin on my neck is crepey, age spots dot my arms and my face. I need to sleep more than ever, and I get tired more easily. I don't have immediate recall of names that I once had, and it's difficult to learn new things (and sometimes I just give up instead of continuing to try). These are all signs of me aging. Is that dreaded nursing home all I have look forward to? Will I not be able to drive or think for myself or even wipe my own butt? Then who will I be? If that's all I have to look forward to, I want no part of it. Is growing old a cruel joke that the Almighty plays on us, his simple creatures—see what you were, see what you might have been, but you're no longer that and you can't have anything more? What lessons have I learned from my visit today? Is it inevitable that I will deteriorate and fade away?

Journal Entry #8

I read over yesterday's entry. It was pretty pessimistic. It seemed like I had already given up on my life, as if I had nothing to look forward to but sadness, frailty and pain. And that's what's at the core of my issue with getting older. I sure hope Michael can help me with this!

There are so many questions that I am wrestling with. Is getting older the beginning of the end or just the end of the beginning? Does growing old have a purpose, some aim, some goal that God set up for the natural process of living? Does the pessimistic attitude that I showed in yesterday's entry reveal that my future is dark and desperate, or is this pessimistic attitude precisely what makes my future seem dark and desperate? Is my approach to getting older itself a sort of self-fulfilling prophecy?

Surely I am slowing down and my bodily functions are not what they once were, but does that mean I'm simply fading away? Could it possibly be that whatever age I might be, if I am realistic about my strengths and weaknesses, I can get as much out of my situation as I can? It seems that with my growing older the less I can run, jump and lift, yet with my growing older the more I do not have to run, jump and lift because with my life experience I can figure out how to get things done in different ways. I might not be as quick at learning a new language as a child, but I can problem solve like no child can. I may not be able to remember what I had for lunch yesterday, but I can remember the date of my wedding and the births of my children and grandchildren, memories that enrich and enliven my days.

So I need to get back to Michael to talk over all I've written about in this journal. It seems that there are always different topics but always one theme: What is the true meaning of my getting older, of my reaching senior status? Is it the end of me or a new way of being me? I keep wondering whether I should dread getting older or should look forward to it.

I wonder why I can't just slide right into this phase of my life. Sometimes I wish I were a slug. Then I would just glide along the earth without a care in the world. At other times I'm glad to be a human being because there is vitality and excitement in dealing with challenges. Without the pull of gravity a body withers away; without the pull of personal challenges I wither away. Use it or lose it. Maybe the growth that challenges bring is different at my age than when I was younger. Although my life surely is different now, that does not mean it is less. What I really need is guidance as to how I can keep growing in terms of a purpose for getting older.

But I can't be the only one who has ever felt this way. Others must have asked what does being older mean. If so, what would that look like? I can just imagine ...

Part II: Chapter Eight

(DON'S STORY ABOUT THE MEANING OF GETTING OLDER)

THE ROUNDTABLE

Sally's Diner was more than just a restaurant. It was the community meeting center where town folk came to start and nurture friendships. It was a place that was especially popular with the senior-citizen population. It had a goodly number of round tables with red-and-white checker-board oil cloth table coverings. These tables could easily accommodate four to eight people facing one another so that no one felt left out or slighted.

Sally's was the monthly meeting place of five senior men who had been having breakfast and coffee together for six years now. They had shared their joys and their sorrows, their successes and their failures, their questions and their answers. Some people go to barbershops for this kind of camaraderie, some to bars and some to counseling sessions. Sam, Ken, Larry, Jim and Ralph went to Sally's. Their routine meetings were more than a habit; they were a ritual. Attendance was praised and absence noted and cared about. All five were retirees from one profession or another. Sam had worked as a long-haul truck driver. Ken was a retired dentist. Larry and Jim had worked together at the local auto plant and retired when the plant became too automated for their liking. Ralph was a retired federal investigator who had re-invented himself as a life coach. All five of them were aware that their work histories were varied and that some of the work they did required more education than others. But that had no bearing on their relationship. To their minds they were all just ordinary guys living one day at a time. As Sam was fond of saying, "I don't give a crap about what you did or how much money you made. I just care about you showing up and how you treat me." He summed up the group's approach very well.

It was Friday, and that meant it was time to share coffee and breakfast at Sally's. The round table in the back corner was reserved for the little group. It even had a sign on it that said "RESERVED." The five were expected by 10 am, and on this day they began to arrive one-by-one around the same time as they had done now for six straight years. They were faithful to one another, so there was always a concern when one of them was absent. And on this day Jim failed to appear.

"Let's wait a little while longer," suggested Larry. He had worked with Jim for about ten years and knew it was not like him to be a "no show."

"Well, let's at least get going on the coffee while we're waiting," suggested Ralph.

"Good call," chimed in Ken as he waved their usual waitress over to their table.

The consensus was that they would wait a short while, decide what they wanted to have for breakfast, and at least start the get-together with good, hot coffee. It was not long before Doris, a middle-age light-haired waitress with ruby red lipstick and a white uniform, came to their table with a pot of coffee and started to fill their ceramic cups as she had so many times before. "Do you'all know what you're havin' this bright, sunny mornin'? Should I bring the regular for each of you strong, han'some gents, or you wanna try somethin' new today?"

"We're going to wait to order, Doris. Jim's not here yet, and we don't want to eat our food without him. It shouldn't be too long. But keep the coffee coming," said Ken as he raised his half-full cup so she could give him a warm-up.

"Anything else before I leave?" asked Doris. The men shook their heads. Doris looked at them all and smiled. "Well, you just call me over when you all are ready, OK?" The group smiled back with an expression of appreciation and agreement. Doris walked away with the now almost empty coffee pot.

Larry looked at his watch and noted with concern in his voice, "It's just not like him, you know, especially since he didn't call any of us. I hope nothing's wrong. Tell you what. Let me call him and see what the holdup is." Larry reached for his cellphone and dialed Jim's number, but there was no answer. "That's funny," noted Larry with a bit of alarm in his voice. "Let me try again." And he did, but this time Jim answered. His voice was uncharacteristically soft, and he answered, "Hello," with hesitation.

"Hey, Buddy, it's Larry. Did you forget today's Friday? We're all here but you. What's going on?"

"I was going to call you, but I fell back to sleep and forgot all about it. I don't know what's gotten into me lately. I'm always tired, I'm always forgetful and I can't shake the sadness."

"About Jenny?"

"It was so sudden, Larry. I can't seem to get over it. We were planning on a world tour. We were real excited about it. Then she has a heart attack right here in this room. I tried to revive her but couldn't. I couldn't save my love. Now I miss her so much. It's like my heart is broke in two. In fact I can't talk about it anymore. I'm going to hang up now. Tell the fellas I'm sorry. I just can't do it anymore." Then Jim put the phone down and Larry was left hanging and wondering what would become of his long-time friend.

"He's not coming," Larry announced to the rest of the group. "Says he got up and fell back to sleep. I must have woken him up with my second call. He didn't sound too good, like the wind is out of his sails. Seems pretty broken up about Jenny."

Ken took a sip of coffee then looked at Larry and said, "Can't really blame him, can you? They were supposed to celebrate their 50th on a tour, but, wham!, she goes and has a heart attack, and now he feels all alone."

Sam joined in. "He seemed OK at the funeral. Talked with everyone. Showed his appreciation that we all showed up."

"I guess that's typical," added Ralph. "It's all OK when there's a lot of people around. But, damn, it must be really hard when you get back home and realize there's no one else there. And there never will be again. 'Never more,' quoth the raven."

Ken was clearly worried about Jim. "I went to see him a couple of days after the funeral. You know, to see how he was doing. He seemed all right although he was distracted and couldn't focus. But I haven't seen or heard from him for about two weeks now. Wonder if I should just drop by."

Ralph thought that might help Jim feel less isolated. "What he's doing is not hiding from us but grieving and figuring out how to go on without Jenny."

"That scares me," noted Ken with a grimace. "I heard that it's old males like us that are more likely to commit suicide than any other group. That includes guys like Jim who have lost their way. He and Jenny were really close. They went everywhere together, and since he retired they did a lot together. They didn't seem to get on each other's nerves. They liked being together. I guess like they were before they had kids. Jim's really struggling without his soulmate."

"Maybe he's lost his way," said Sam.

"Maybe he's lost himself," added Ralph.

Always the practical one, Sam suggested that they order their breakfasts before poor Doris slipped them lunch menus. Although they wanted to continue their discussion, all four of the friends held on to what they were thinking and gave Doris a wave.

"What's it gonna be, boys?" Their appetites were doused by their conversation, but they all ordered something. The group then continued their heavy conversation.

"I don't think we have to worry about Jim doing anything stupid. His daughter checks on him every day, and if she finds anything funny, she'll take care of it," Ken said.

"It still bothers me," noted Ralph, "that a guy like Jim would be sinking into the rabbit hole. But what bugs me even more is that sometimes I get the feeling that now that I'm older and not working, it would be easier to slip down that hole than fight to keep going."

"I know what you mean," said Sam. "Sometimes I just get tired of fighting. I mean, when I was younger I welcomed challenges. But then I had a reason to meet them. I had a family to take care of. I had a job to keep going to. I had a future that I wanted to be better than my dad's."

"You know," continued Sam, "he got old and then seemed to stop. He was sixty-five, I think it was, and he left his job as a mechanic because he didn't want the hassles anymore. He just quit the job, collected his pension and social security, and sat. Watched TV all day. He hardly went out of the house. Sure he played with my kids when we came over to visit, but he never went out of his way to visit us or go travelling with my mom or do anything other than sit in front of that damn TV set or sit on the porch. Worked around the house but he never made the house better. My mother would get so mad at him. She called him a 'lump.' But he didn't seem to care. He told her to stop nagging him. That he was coasting, just coasting."

Sam paused thoughtfully. The rest of the group noticed he was getting agitated and his remarks coming out forcefully. Sam went on saying, "I really don't think I want to live like that. You can't just 'coast.' When you coast, you're toast. I could see that my dad was kind of just wasting away. But that's not me. I know that Jim had a gut punch when Jenny died so suddenly. He's grieving. Got it. But my dad acted as if he died when he retired. He said he stopped working because he was 'too old for this crap.' But then he got old fast.

"You know, we're all senior citizens. But are we old old? Can't we be young old? Jim's loss sure is a kick-in-the-ass, but I've seen others like my dad who tumble down that rabbit hole even without the passing of a loved one."

As Sam finished his monologue, Doris came over to the table with a large tray stacked with the group's breakfast orders. Silence had come over the four men. Noticing this and finding it uncharacteristic of the group, Doris took it upon herself to both serve up the meals and serve up some observations.

"Here's your orders, gents. But I must say I've never seen this group in such a glum mood. No jokes, no stories, no laughter. Come on, guys, get it together. The sun's out, the food's good and you're all together again."

All four reached out to handle their orders, and as the plates were passed around, Ralph looked up at Doris and said, "We've been discussing some pretty heavy-duty stuff. I think now would be a really good time to hear one of your famous bad Doris jokes."

Doris was very pleased to hear that she had the power to lighten the group's mood. So after all the plates were passed and the coffee cups refilled, Doris set the coffee pot and the empty tray down on the table and stood in front of the group as if she were the star attraction. They all turned toward her with rapt attention.

"Did you hear the one about the large beef stick that goes into a bar looking angry? The bartender stares at him and says, 'Don't look at me that way. I've got no beef with you.'"

A collective light-hearted groan went up from the group. "That's so bad, it's funny," remarked Ken. "Got another one?"

Doris was tickled pink that they wanted more, so she dished up one of her favorites.

"Did you hear the one about the large millipede that walks into a bar and orders a drink. The bartender asks, 'Are you over 21?' 'No,' says the bug, 'I'm over 100.'"

This joke got everyone chuckling but Sam who didn't get it. But then he slapped his forehead and said, "I just got it! It's a play on the word 'over.' I really must be getting old. A little slow on the uptake."

He looked at Doris and said, "Thanks for raising our spirits, Doris. You're just what the doctor ordered."

This comment pleased Doris to no end. "That's all folks!" she said light-heartedly. "I'll be here all morning. Don't forget to tip your waitress."

Sam spoke up. "Thanks. We needed that, Sweetheart. That's why we like coming here."

Doris smiled and walked away. The group then focused on their meals until Sam spoke up. "That Doris sure is something. I don't know how she's always upbeat. She's got to be sixty-five years old if she's a day. What's her secret?"

"Whatever it is, I ain't got it," remarked Larry. "And you know why I ain't got it? It's because I'm pissed off that I seem to be breaking down. I've had two knee replacements so I can't play baseball or tennis like I used to. I seem to have some arthritis in my hips, so I can't bend down except with effort. I did some painting at my son's house the other day, and when I got home I hurt all over because of stepping up and down on the ladder and the twisting I did to get into the nooks and crannies.

"And that's not all. Every day I take a pill for my blood pressure. I take a statin for my heart, and I take a pill to keep my macular degeneration from getting worse. You know, I never had to take pills like this before. I never had to sleep as much as I do, recuperate as long as I have to, watch what I eat as much, be careful not to slip and fall as much. Remember when we used to go out starting at 10 pm and make a night of it? Now I'm usually in bed by 9:30! And I like to have a blanket over my legs when I read or watch TV. Just like those old guys with the beautiful young women that marry them for their money. Am I turning into an 'old guy'? And worst of all sometimes I dribble, and I don't mean a basketball. Am I going to need diapers?"

The group laughed knowingly at this question. Then Ken put down his coffee cup and said, "I know exactly what you mean, my friend. But it has affected me also in the bedroom. Remember when you could perform daily?" The rest of group smiled knowingly. "Well, I can't seem to get it up more than once or twice a month, and then Lynn has to help a lot. Don't get me wrong. When we get it on, it's great. Maybe even better than when we were younger because we don't have to worry about her getting pregnant. But I feel less manly when I can't be ready whenever I want to. I don't want to take a pill or go to some clinic even though my performance sometimes is no performance at all. And that makes me embarrassed and frustrated. Never been like this before."

"Has Lynn's craving for sex changed as well?" asked Ralph. "Phyllis seems detached from sex. She would rather just hold hands, go for walks and have long talks. What is it with women our age? Does their sex drive just fade away after they have children and raise them? It bothers me to think that sometimes when we make love she just goes along with it because she thinks she has to or she's trying to be nice to me. I don't want a mother or a caretaker! I want a partner like the way it used to be."

Sam added in between forkfuls, "I can't speak for how women feel about senior sex, but I know someone who can. Let's get Doris back over her. Maybe she can enlighten us from the female point of view."

"Doris!" Sam called out. "Could you come over here for a minute, and bring the coffee pot with you?"

"Be right there," Doris replied.

Doris sauntered over to the table in good spirits expecting the group to ask her to lighten their mood once again. She had no idea what was in store for her. And when she came to the table, Ralph asked her to pull up a chair. Then she was put on the spot.

Sam began. "Doris we've been talking about what it's like to get old. And we need some female input. You're married, right?"

"Some forty-three years last month."

"Has love making changed for you and your husband over the years since you're both older now?"

Doris was taken aback by the brazenness of the question, but because she felt comfortable with the group, she smiled a wily smile and answered as if she were an expert on the subject.

"Boys, my Jess and me have five kids, so believe me, we know what we're doin' when it comes to gettin' together. We were hot as pistols when we first married, but we slowed down when the children came. We picked up again after they all finally scooted from home. And now we approach the whole subject of gettin' together like a slow cooker.

"Now I've overheard men talk about their frustration with not having as much sex as they had earlier in their marriages. That makes me laugh. Did you ever see little kids running around the schoolyard at recess? They scream and they run, and they don't go nowhere. They're just burnin' off that youngin type of energy. But it's all wasted. It's like a dam that's busted. The water bursts out every which way with no purpose or goal. It don't do no one any good because it's just energy on the loose."

Doris stopped for a moment to be sure her audience was still with her. They were. She had them wrapped around her little finger. So she went on. "I guess sex is like that, boys. When you're young, you're like a dam that bursts. It needs to get out every which way. But when you get older, like everything else, you realize that it all needs to be controlled and directed. At one point it's directed toward children. But what about when you can't have kids anymore? It's not that there's no more energy; it's that it's directed to something else. You see, me and Jesse don't get it on as much anymore, but when we do it's wonderful. It's not a relief of pent-up energy; it's more a being together for no other reason than that. Being together. It makes us happy to be together after all these years. Thank God for being older. Don't think I could've appreciated Jesse as much when I was younger. Senior sex is different than junior sex. It's not a matter of more or less times, but of more or less closeness. The secret is that old people sex can be better than young people sex. That's cuz both of you bring more to it, so you get more out of it."

The four men were stunned with Doris's response. They spontaneously clapped and cheered.

"That deserves a monumental tip," declared Sam.

"Here's a tip: Get a degree in counseling," joked Ken.

Doris blushed and said, "Well, if you fellas don't need me anymore, I have a few other customers to take care of. Oops! Now don't take that the wrong way." Then Doris just sauntered away with a big smile on her face.

As the men were finishing their breakfasts, Ken smacked the table and muttered, "Damn, I forgot them again!"

"Forgot what?" asked Sam

"My pills. Like the rest of you, I have a mini-tackle box of meds, but I don't put my supplements in that box, so I forget to take them. Too many details. I can't remember them all."

"What do you take?" asked Ralph.

"Organic compounds for my skin, compounds for maintaining my weight, general daily vitamins and one special one to keep my mental capacity on track. I sure need that one because I've seen some decline in my thinking capacity. Oh, I remember how to fill a tooth and extract a tooth and evaluate general oral health. That's stored in my long-term memory. But my short-term memory seems like a sieve rather than a lockbox."

"Like why you walked into a room?" asked Larry.

"Like where you put the hammer?" added Sam.

"Like what she asked you to do?" quipped Ralph.

"Like each of you said." Ken chuckled. "Since I'm no longer a practicing dentist, I try to keep up my mental sharpness by playing some computer games, doing sudokus and trying my hand at crossword puzzles. I've even been learning Spanish."

"And how's that working for you?" asked Ralph.

"Well, like I said, I still have my general dentistry knowledge pretty well intact, although without being active in the field I'm sure my skills and knowledge of short-cuts aren't what they were a few years ago. My problem is with details. Names, dates, even what I had for supper yesterday. Sometimes I can't even find my car keys.

"Now I've tried to get myself in routines that become habits so I don't have to think about what to do. And I make myself notes. I jot down my thoughts, because, you know, they seem to fade soon after they appear. I just hate it when I have a good idea, and then it slips away from me. Sometimes I can get it back, but not directly. I have to wait, and later it mysteriously reappears." Ken hesitated as if he were recalling a long-lost friend then said, "And all this has happened since I became a senior. I can handle it, at least for now, but it kind of worries me."

"Dementia?" Larry asked.

"Especially Altheimer's," Ken confirmed. "I know that most of the stuff I'm experiencing is pretty characteristic of the aging brain, but I'm always asking myself if this time what's happening is not just a change in my brain, but a deterioration of it. I'm afraid that all my life experience and professional expertise will eventually fade away like my fleeting ideas. Then it will not be just my thoughts that vanish but my ability to think. And if I lose all I've gained throughout my life, I might revert back to my childhood, and I don't want to be taken care of, to do things that are odd and disgusting, to be unable to recognize those I love, and eventually to even forget who I am. That's my greatest fear when it comes to getting older, fellas. To have all I've done, all I've hoped for, all I am, taken from me—while I'm still alive. I hate to say this, but I'd rather be dead than be like that!"

Ken teared up at the thought, and the group fell silent once again. Then Larry put his arm around Ken's shoulder and said, "Cheer up, Buddy. Anyone who can explain his fears as well as you have just now ain't even close to being out of it."

"Yeah, if having Alzheimer's helps me to say what you just said, then I say let me have some … Now what did I just say?" Sam smiled a sly smile, feeling a bit guilty for his dark humor.

Ken blurted out, "It's no laughing matter, Sammy! We should all be aware that as we get older, we move closer to the decline of our lives. We have to face the fact that death and dementia loom on the horizon. I'm really afraid of what might happen to me." Ken fell silent.

Just then with impeccable timing Doris returned to the table with her customary coffee pot. "More coffee? And will that be all, Professors?"

"You know just when to appear, don't you?" replied Ralph. "I think some of us could use a little more coffee and then we can take our checks."

Doris laid the four checks on the table, and before anyone else reached for theirs, Ralph took them all. "Put them all on my credit card, Doris. I may be getting older, but I've not lost my appreciation for these guys, no matter how ugly they are."

"Thanks a lot," said Sam.

"Much appreciated," added Larry.

"That was very kind of you," noted Ken as Ralph's gesture seemed to soothe his troubled heart.

Then Ralph spoke up trying to change the focus of the conversation. He said, "Fellas, I understand that we have only so much time left on this planet. But I can't see spending it worrying about what could go wrong or how short it might be. I've been thinking about this long and hard, and I wonder if the meaning of getting older is really about how best to live our lives while we still have them."

Larry jumped in enthusiastically. "You know, I think living as an elder includes a certain sensitivity to our lives, an attitude that seems to just sneak up on you as you get to our age. I'm beginning to think that as seniors we put less stock in doing what we must do and more stock in doing what we want to do. We find ourselves enjoying life because we can feel free from the bonds of needs and duties."

"You know, that's exactly why I left my dental practice," noted Ken. "Day in and day out I went to the office, did what I had to do, then went home and Lynn and I would go out or stay home—and then I'd do it all over again the next day. I looked forward to the weekend. But then I decided to have some weekend hours for my patients, and then weekends became like weekdays. And when I wasn't working at the office, I was working at home and then resting from work trying to relax enough to sleep—and do it all over again. I knew I was doing good for people and I enjoyed meeting the challenges each patient's situation presented, but it eventually became a drudgery. I no longer wanted to be driven by routine and obligation."

Larry jumped in saying, "That's what I'm talking about. Clock in; clock out. Projects to be completed, orders to fill, and there's always pressure to do the work faster, cheaper, better. I was grateful I had a job to support my family. But then I realized I didn't enjoy the work as much as I used to, and my sons were earning their own paychecks—thank God. So I began to detach from my work, and I began to care less and less about it. My performance dipped and my supervisor asked me what was going on. I couldn't tell her the truth that I didn't give a damn any more for fear of losing my job, so I just said I was sorry. That's all she wanted to hear, and she reminded me to stay as productive as I usually was and to be the outstanding employee I had always been.

"But I eventually couldn't see my way to doing over and over again what was becoming more and more a pain in the ass. So I knew the time had come to move on. I was old enough to retire with a fine pension, so I put in for retirement, and I've never looked back.

"I escaped a joyless landscape, but I haven't found anything to replace it with yet. My house is paid for, my finances are set, my children are grown, my health is reasonably fine. And I keep telling myself I've got it pretty good, yet I feel kinda lost. My whole life has been a search for security in the face of all the challenges that life poses. I lived my life to do and to have. Well, I've done a lot and I have a lot. So I ask, now what? Like Ken, I needed to escape from drudgery, but I'm unclear what that turns me toward. I'm no longer satisfied with my past, yet I'm uncertain about my future. Here I am free from what I felt bound to do when I was younger, yet I don't quite know what my elder freedom is for."

Larry seemed to be speaking for the group as a whole at this point. The other three were paying close attention to what he was saying. So he went on explaining that "When I started my retirement, I was naïve enough to think that now I could just sail through life on a plateau of happiness. But it's not that way. I'm experiencing a sort of an elder adolescence. I'm not happy. I'm adrift. I keep asking what am I to do with myself now? Who am I now that I'm not working? And I've begun to suspect that my hard work and struggle for all those years may have been worth it to support myself and my family, but my busyness had at the same time been a distraction from what might be the real point of my life. Now I'm face-to-face with the question: What is my life really all about? And I keep hearing a little voice saying to me, 'So what? So what?'"

It was Ralph who then spoke up. "It seems to me that Larry's concerns are all our concerns. We're at a point in our lives when we are asking a most important question—what are we to do now? We're not about what we were before. Well, what I'm thinking is that we might learn something from Maslow's ideas on human development."

"You must be alluding to Maslow's theory on the stages of human development that's always part of Psychology 101," clarified Ken.

"Right on, my friend. It accounts for the five basic needs of every human being."

"And they are …?" asked Sam.

"First, physiological needs. These are the requirements for base survival like food, water, and air. Safety and security needs come next. These are whatever keeps us from danger and produce a sense of calm. Love and belonging needs follow. Human beings need to be appreciated and cared for. The need for a sense of self-esteem is next."

"But that's only four," noted Larry.

Ralph appreciated this comment, for it made him feel like the guys were really listening, and he wasn't just lecturing. So he continued saying, "Precisely, Larry. And that's because the first four needs are essentially different from the fifth need that Maslow calls self-actualization.

"The first four are all about my own shortcomings. They arise from deficiencies in my life that need to be remedied. I need to acquire these things in order to survive and thrive. But what happens when human beings have had these four needs filled? Do they just sit down on a rocking chair and wait to die? Absolutely not! There often now comes a deep dis-satisfaction concerning one's life, the kind of being lost feeling we're experiencing. It's the sense that my being OK is not good enough. There's more to my life than just feeling OK. There's a discomfort with achieving all we have, and it's the nagging question of what this feeling of being OK implies. Is it that we are supposed to just sit back and bask in our achievements? Or do our personal cups 'runneth over' to get us to share our fullness with the rest of the world?

"You know, satisfying the first four needs may not be the end goal of life. Getting them satisfied may really be meant to set up a platform for caring for something beyond ourselves. It's like, we human beings, when we have enough to eat, have our homes, are financially stable, have a family and are accomplished at our employments, we become ready to reach out to something else without being motivated by what we can get out of it."

Ralph looked over at Larry and said, "I think that's what you're dealing with. Your platform has been built, and you're wondering, 'Now what?' You no longer have to seek what you don't have. You've got what you need. But that's not enough to make your life satisfying. That's because you're ready for self-actualization. You long to reach out into the world and make an impact, leave a legacy. Your newfound sense of freedom is prompting you to create art, perform community service, share your wisdom. You long to focus your freedom and your power to change the world for the better without thinking about how it will profit you."

Ralph stopped and noticed that his friends were quite attentive, but they still had quizzical looks on their faces as if they did not fully understand what he was saying. So Ralph continued on. "Now you may say, what you're talking about is stuff we've already done. But I say it may look like it's the same thing, but it's not. A self-actualized act is one done without yourself in mind. It's selfless. It's done out of appreciation, wonder, hope for the future. Self-actualized action is more like play than work. What you've been doing is well and good, even necessary to take care of yourselves and your families, but it's been about getting and having while self-actualization is more about creativity and awe and reverence."

Ralph took a sip of coffee to catch his breath. Then he went on saying, "Probably a good way to explain this is the matter of religion. There are many people in this world who practice a religion, but I dare say there are few that practice it the way it is meant to be practiced. Most people use religion to get things—fortune, security, fame. They believe in God as a power to fill gaps in themselves, other people and the world around them. If they think that God is 'not on their side,' is not favoring them with what they want and need, they will reject faith as useless. They use religion to 'get' what they can't get on their own.

"But religion, like self-actualization, is really a state of grace, a being filled with a power which enables people to perform acts not to gain profit nor to please, but to reverence and care for and build up. Teachers can teach for the money or teachers can teach out of love for their students. The first is motivated by the first four needs; the second by self-actualization."

Ralph leaned forward to emphasize his final point. "Fellas, this pertains so much to our situations and what growing old may be all about. We need to stop picking flowers to sell them or collect them in a vase. We need to just dance among them singing and praising all that is good! If I were a lyricist I might write a song for people our age about playing in the world for the pure joy of it."

No one spoke when Ralph finished. He seemed to have touched everyone's heart.

Right on cue, Doris arrived with the credit card slip for Ralph. Everyone at the table looked up and put on a smile. "Have yourselves a good day now, boys," she said. "Hope to see you soon. Oh, and by the way, me and Jesse are goin' on a date tonight. And you betcha it's gonna be a humdinger!" Then she winked and walked away whistling a happy tune.

Ralph signed the slip giving Doris a very generous tip. Then he resumed the conversation hoping to tie everything together quickly before they all left for home. "So what I'm saying is that moving into senior status might be meant to get us ready to escape a self-centered way of life. Its purpose may be to propel us into a way of life that's not about us and about what we can get. It's about being free to selflessly share all we are and have."

Ralph drained his coffee cup and resumed with one last thought. "Maybe it's like our relationship here at this table. I don't give a rat's ass what your employment situation was or where you live or how much money you have in the bank. How you are here and now to me and to the rest of us, that's all that matters. I guess getting older can be like having a new start. Being older is not supposed to be about casting off our old selves, but about morphing them into a different way of being ourselves. Free and selfless."

The group was silent for a moment then Sam chimed in with a question that was bothering him. "What then exactly am I supposed to do if I'm self-actualized? Now that I'm retired, I have lots of time on my hands. How should I spend that time? I'm so used to spending the bulk of my time at work or in bed."

Larry answered Sam's question by grabbing his jacket from the back of his seat and saying as he put it on, "As for me I think I'm going to use my time visiting Jim. It would be a good thing to do, and I'm going to do it for no other reason than he really needs someone there for him right now."

"Maybe that's what Ralph's been talking about," suggested Sam.

"Maybe so," responded Larry. "In any case, thank you all for your company this beautiful morning. And I thank you for what you've given me to think about too. Damn, what a time it was! See you in about a month."

Ralph chimed in, "Looking forward to it," and the others nodded in agreement.

Larry smiled at the group as he left the restaurant and the others smiled back. The other three remained at the table for a little while to let what had occurred during the last two hours sink in. Then they stood up and shook hands with each other saying, "Till next time!"

Watching them leave the restaurant, Doris felt a warm glow. They had treated her as much more than a walking coffee dispenser. That made her smile inside, and for a long time.

Man, I would've fit right in with those guys! I'm going through the same stuff. But am I really in a fresh and better place?

Part II: Chapter Nine

(JOURNAL ENTRIES #9 & #10)

Journal Entry #9

I've only got a couple days left till I see Michael again. He's a really nice guy, but I wonder if he really understands what I'm going through since he's much younger than I. Yet as I think about it, so is my doctor and my dentist, all younger than me. But they're good at what they do. Does chronological age really matter? Can you be good at what you do and have wisdom even though you're not a senior citizen? Of course you can! What's wrong with me?

I've caught myself arguing with myself with this journaling. I may not be figuring things out, but I'm at least getting clear in my old brain what issues I need to be dealing with concerning my getting up there in years. Like spending my time. I need to get this one thing straight in my mind and in my heart so I can see my way clear to how I should live the rest of my life. Of course I've been wondering about "the rest of my life" ever since I was a kid. It's just that now "the rest of my life" appears as a shorter period of time than ever before and with fewer options. And as I think about it, isn't that what I've been trying to figure out all along? What to do with the time I have left. If I'm going to make my time worthwhile, I had better get to it since my time is limited. No procrastination for me. It's more like "now or never." And maybe that's a good thing because I can't put it off any longer. I need to face it head on because it's already facing me, and if I don't get to it, something will, and it may be something out of my control.

So the major issue is how should I spend my time till my literal deadline.

That's what happens when you stop working a job. You have more time on your hands than you can imagine. I've always had time on my hands, but I always filled it with doing things to gain stuff or maintain my stuff or protect my stuff. No longer the case. I feel sorry for those who come to my age and are still struggling to survive till the next day. I don't have that problem. Got it—house, pensions, children, all those things I have been working to get. The question is: Now that I have all these things, what do I do with my time? Play, play, play? Detach from work so much that all I do all day long is spend my time on leisure activities? Golf, TV, bowling, cruises. Is that what retirement and old age is all about--escaping the drudgery of the work world by refusing to work at anything at all? Is this later time of my life simply a reward for my hard work, so that all I need do is reap the fruits of my labor?

But I have a problem with that. Take astronauts. If they give in to the weightlessness of outer space, they become flabby. They lose muscle tone, and with the loss of muscle tone, they cannot move about to get their work done. It's like being confined to a hospital bed. Lay long enough and you find it difficult to get out of bed and get around. Atrophy sets in. All of this is because it seems we're made to face challenges even if it's as simple as gravity. It keeps pulling us down. So if we want to keep standing, we must continue to fight it, and the more we fight gravity the stronger we become, like with strength training.

I don't want to become a blob on the earth. I want to be strong and vibrant, so I need to use my time to do something, not just sit back and relax. When I speak of the rest of my life, I don't look forward to resting for the remainder of my life. The remainder of my life needs to be meaningful, worthwhile, interesting. Not doing something, not working toward something is BORING. And when I get bored, I get anxious and depressed, signs that I need to get off my duff and engage my world and those in it. I need to spend my time investing in life, not burying my life in the ground hoping that at least I won't lose what time I have left.

Wow! See what Michael's got me doing. This is the best entry I've ever done. Getting better with practice. But this is enough. I already feel a headache coming on. So I'm sure being older is all about spending time meaningfully. Now I have to figure just what is a meaningful way to spend the time left to me.

Journal Entry #10

I have only so much time left. My question is: Is getting older a death sentence or a life opportunity? Has my life taken me this far for me to realize that there's nothing left? Or has my life prepared me for what I am to do and be for the remainder of my life? If there's not much to look forward to but biding my time till I die, that's depressing. But if I'm now more ready than ever for a new lease on life, that's exciting.

Sometimes I find dead flies on my windowsills. Apparently they just died, faded away. Nothing more to say. Is getting older merely a process of fading away? If so, I should stop and let it happen because there's nothing I can do about. But I'm not so sure now. I know there's nothing I can do about dying, but surely there's something I can do about the life I lead till then. And won't the kind of life I lead until I die say something about the meaning of my death?

I refuse to just fade. It's disrespectful to myself. I'm so much more than a fly. But how should I approach what is left of my life? That's the question! To be involved in something for the rest of my life I need to have a purpose and a plan. An arrow does not hit its target unless it is propelled with force and accuracy. I need to know where my arrow is to go. What should I be about? Why continue to live if I'm going to die anyway? The continuing on must be worth it. What makes it worth it? How do I find this worth and how do I bring it to flower?

I'm not done cultivating the world with my life. I just don't know how I should do it. And I don't know how I should do it because I can't quite get what becoming a senior is for. I know that I have more time on my hands than ever before. Is it for having this time that I've come to this stage of my life? If that's so, what's the difference in this time and the time I had before when I was trying to achieve goals that got me to where I'm at now?

It seems that my later years are a different kind of time for me. What is this time calling me to do, to be? Maybe it's a special time. Like wedding time and birthing time and graduation time. These were times when I was filled with joy. I just lived them, basked in them. Is my elder time like those times? This time is certainly not about inaction. Maybe it's about a different kind of action.

I'm wondering whether I should be glad that I'm "older." Maybe the time I have left is for finally exploring and engaging the deepest meanings of my life now that I'm not distracted by worry about getting, keeping and protecting my stuff.

But I can't be the only one who has ever felt this way. Others must have thought about time and how best to spend it. If so, what would that look like? I can just imagine …

Part II: Chapter Ten

(DON'S STORY ABOUT SPENDING TIME)

In a Moment

Robynn bent over the glass case intent upon finding the precise instrument she was looking for. She had very high standards when it came to time pieces. These were all lovely time pieces, but where they chronometer worthy? For Robynn it was not the look of the time piece nor its status nor its brand but its absolute accuracy. Time mattered to her more than anything else. She had been an efficiency expert for many years now. Currently she was a consultant for an international delivery service which stressed being on time all the time. There was no time to waste, so they looked to Robynn to polish their current delivery methods and recommend how to be even more efficient in the process--because time was money.

Robynn pointed to a gold watch and asked if it was COSC certified. The salesclerk looked at her like a deer caught in a car's headlights. "COSC certified?" he asked.

"Yes, COSC certified. That means it's certified by the Swiss Chronometer Institute to be within +6 to -4 seconds a day accurate. Every other watch is just a piece of jewelry."

"Well, I don't know whether it's certified that way," said the salesclerk, "but it has a lot of great features. It tells the day and date, the time to the second and includes a timer and stopwatch. I'd have to check with my manager if it's certified."

"There's no need. I'm an efficiency expert, so measuring time and trying to control it is what I do all day every day. I guess I just like to look at time pieces. Time pieces like these are more than just watches. They're like miniature artworks that require the craft of a master. For me time pieces are symbols of life because they measure time, and time is the movement of life. Time is the most important commodity in life. Without it, there is no life; with it, a person can prosper. That's why I'm an efficiency expert. I help people not to waste precious time. As the old saying goes, 'Tempus fugit, time flies.' People should be very aware of how they spend their time because time is like water. It can be your friend, but it can be your enemy as well. Anyway, don't bother consulting your manager. I'm more just admiring your selection rather than shopping for another watch. Thank you for your time."

Robynn walked out of the store and headed for the exit of the mall where she had met with two friends for lunch, which was rather uncharacteristic of Robynn because she was a rather introverted person, preferring to take measurements and work on efficiency plans rather than spend her time frivolously. And that is how she felt about meeting friends for lunch. It was a nice break, but it was essentially a waste of time. Like always, she talked with her friends about what she considered mundane matters. They joked and they laughed, and they gave updates on their situations, but they did not solve any problems and did not come up with any consequential plans. Robynn had developed a persona that was cordial but strictly business. She did not have time for the trivial.

As she walked out of the mall, Robynn began to think about her current project to streamline the delivery company's service to island communities in the South Pacific. It was a pet project of hers, one that would greatly feed her already stellar reputation. She was proud of her devotion to the management of time. Her work was very important because it meant people could be dynamic and productive rather than static and dependent on forces other than themselves. That was dangerous. Personal freedom and dignity were grounded in a person's approach to time. Waste your time; waste your life.

Robynn was happy with her life, and she was even more satisfied with it when she walked up to her silver and blue smart car in the mall parking lot. *Buying this car was a master stroke*, she thought. Here was efficiency molded into a vehicle that not only was economically priced but got her wherever she wanted to go for less.

She unlocked the car and threw her purse on the passenger seat in the front. But then she had a disturbing thought. *Today was Friday, and wasn't she supposed to meet with the director of the company to review her proposals for the South Pacific project? It was!* The prim, proper and always punctual Robynn had forgotten about the meeting. *Why didn't my watch alert me to the meeting?* The meeting was at 1:00 pm in the director's office in the company's corporate headquarters located thirty minutes away, and it was already 12:25 pm. She had to arrive on time if she were to impress the director and convince him to accept her recommendations. It worried her that she had only five minutes to spare, and if there was traffic or a lot of stop lights on the way she might not make it on time. She was never late. Robynn prided herself on her punctuality. In fact she usually left for a meeting earlier than necessary to be there on time and be able to freshen up and review what she was going to do at the meeting. But this was too close for comfort, and the meeting was too important to be late for. A tardy efficiency expert. Absurd—and untrustworthy.

So Robynn focused intently on getting to the meeting on time. She started the car as quickly as she could and pulled away from her parking spot with a vengeance. And with her panic mode combined with her laser-like focus on getting to the meeting on time, she neglected to put on her seatbelt. She never did that before; never had to because she never allowed herself to spend time just admiring things, like the time pieces that she had so enjoyed looking over. *How silly she had been!* Admiring things took precious time away from getting to what she needed to do. She derided herself for indulging in precisely what she helped others avoid, wasting time.

Robynn drove her car as fast as she could through the parking lot until she came to the exit where she was stopped by a traffic light that seemed to be red forever. Then when she was released from its clutches, Robynn took off like a streak from the mall area to the main road. She raced along the road until she approached a four-way-stop that was five minutes from where the director was waiting. *It's not that far now,* she thought trying to comfort herself.

She was intent upon getting to the meeting on time, focused on the road ahead of her, trying to be faithful to her credo of perfect time management. So as she came upon the four-way stop, she did not notice the much larger car racing toward the intersection from her left. She needed to get to the meeting, and this was just a stupid intersection outside of town, probably put there by some politician that got some kickback from a stop sign company. No reason to be there. It was in her way. Yet she did not want to just plow into the intersection, so she did a rolling stop and proceeded through without looking right or left. She did not notice the car rushing into the same intersection at the same time she was passing through. The driver was texting while driving and did not pay attention to the stop sign or the tiny car already in the intersection.

So the larger car slammed full force into Robynn's smart car which had no defenses against such a forceful encounter. The larger car rammed into the smart car like a Roman galley ramming into an enemy ship. Initially, because she was not anchored in the car by her seatbelt, Robynn was thrown across the front seat and crashed headlong into the passenger side window. But the other driver was not finished with her yet. The force of the crash pushed the small car toward a drainage ditch which ran next to the road. And when the smart car came to the edge of the ditch, it rolled over so that it landed upside down in the ditch—with Robynn still inside and fatefully damaged. The roof had collapsed onto the chassis of the car and pinned Robynn beneath it. She already was bleeding from the shards of glass from the window she had struck, and now she was being crushed and could not breathe.

The other driver stopped his car and ran over to the wreck in the drainage ditch. But his efforts to get Robynn out of the car were to no avail. He could only make a 911 call and hope that the EMT's or firefighters or whoever answered his call could save Robynn's life. But Robynn was already unconscious and was rapidly losing blood and breath. She seemed to be dead already, an untimely and unproductive death.

Robynn woke up in a totally different setting. It was a sunlit meadow of brightly colored flowers with hues so varied she could not remember ever experiencing such variety and brilliance. She found herself lying on her back facing the clear blue sky surrounded by this cavalcade of beauty. She was a bit groggy at first, but then she perked up quickly because the sight was almost as wondrous as a perfectly designed chronometer. There was never any interest in her life for flowers because they just stood there doing nothing, standing still in time when they should have been progressing through it. Yet this scene engaged her deeply, so much so that she teared up and held her breath for a moment. Just for a moment, however, because her instincts told her that she had to move on to get things done rather than just basking in the beauty and fragrance of the meadow.

So Robynn, still dressed in her gray business suit with a blue scarf draped around her neck, stood up and began walking through the meadow hoping to come upon something that might provide her with some indication as to where she was. She was properly dressed and ready to meet the director, but she had to find out how to get to his office.

Robynn kept walking through the meadow that seemed to have no end. Yet just as Robynn was about to give up hope of getting out of the meadow, she came upon a stream of clear water flowing from left to right at a leisurely pace. She saw her reflection in the stream and was surprised at how good she looked. She knelt down on the bank of the stream and gave in to the temptation to drink from it. Cupping her hands, Robynn drew some water and brought it to her lips. It was surprising how refreshing it was. She stood up and tried to follow the path of the stream, which to her surprise led nowhere but back to where she was. The stream was flowing in a perfect circle, always different but always the same. She wondered what kind of place this might be to contain such a strange phenomenon as this.

Here was a meadow with what seemed like an infinite variety of flowers and a stream that went nowhere but flowed, nevertheless. Then she noticed that she was standing on a hillside overlooking a wide expanse covered with trees and circular streams and flowers of every shape and size. *What was she looking at?* she wondered. *Why was she here? Was this a dream?* And as she stood there pondering her plight, a little girl about five years old walked up to her from behind and greeted her with, "Hello! My name is Sarah. What's yours?"

Robynn turned around to see the little girl who was wearing a pink sun dress and a white wide-brimmed hat. The tiny girl's apparel was not surprising to Robynn, but what was surprising was the fact that both of her legs were encased in braces from top to bottom. Yet as the girl came closer to Robynn, she walked as if she were not encumbered by the braces. In fact, after greeting Robynn, and without waiting for an answer, the little girl began dancing around Robynn as if she were celebrating Robynn. Robynn crouched down to be face-to-face with the girl who stopped in front of her. "My name is Robynn, Sweetheart. I'm glad to meet you." Robynn wondered who this lovely little one belonged to and how she came upon Robynn in the first place.

The girl looked directly at Robynn and said, "I'm supposed to show you around. You're new here, so I was sent to help you feel at home as soon as possible."

"Thank you. That would be very nice, Sarah."

Sarah took Robynn by the hand and led her down the hill which had an incline gentle enough to allow them to descend easily to the valley below. When they came to the valley, Robynn was taken aback by how resplendent and luxurious it was. Although the sun was high in the sky, a cool breeze wafted over the area, and it brought with it the smell of ripe vegetation.

Sarah let Robynn take in the scene for a short while and then tugged on her hand so that Robynn would continue to follow her. Robynn had no idea where she was being led, but the vibrant scene and the joy beaming from her little guide's face inspired her to not worry about where she was going but just to let it happen. That was so unlike Robynn whose life had been a matter of planning and measuring and critiquing so that no time would be wasted. But this moment seemed so right. *I'm not sure where I've been, nor am I sure where I'm going, but neither matter for some reason. I'm here now and that seems to be enough,* she thought. So Robynn let Sarah lead her on, trusting that Sarah knew what she was doing and where she was going.

They walked and walked until they came to a clearing where what looked like a large family was having a picnic. They came closer but the family did not appear to notice them, probably because they were totally engrossed in playing games and sharing many succulent dishes spread out on a white tablecloth draped over a long picnic table. As Robynn watched them she could not help but notice that they did nothing but eat and play. They were happy in the present. The moment appeared to be enough for them. And the more Robynn watched, the more she became uncomfortable, not with the family nor with their activities, but with the fact that their activity didn't produce anything. Robynn felt uncomfortable with that because she had always thought that the productive use of time was the essence of what having a good time meant. But this scene was only about play. There was no ulterior purpose for what they did. They seemed happy and content just being with one another and sharing food and fellowship. But fellowship was for group planning according to the gospel of Robynn.

There was little time for small talk, and there was no time for just being together. That was not quality time. It was merely a waste of time.

Sarah sensed that Robynn felt distressed, so she once again tugged on Robynn's hand and took her to another circular stream where they came upon a young woman reading a book. She seemed engrossed in it because she did not look up although Sarah and Robynn stood right behind her. Robynn peeked over the young woman's shoulder and noticed that she was reading what appeared to be a novel, the kind of book Robynn thought was the bane of an industrious life. Why read fiction when there were so many non-fiction works available that could teach a person how to better spend their time? What good was fiction? It only served to take the reader out of time which made the reader waste the time they spent reading. Then with a second glance Robynn realized that the book was not a novel at all but a book of poetry. *Ridiculous!* thought Robynn. *What can you get with poetry? Why spend your time with poetry when you could be learning something that made you better at what you do?* Yet the girl was smiling and serene. This did not make any sense to Robynn, because she had always prided herself in her no-nonsense demeanor and her habitual discontent with the present. To her the present was only a steppingstone to what lay ahead in the future. Keeping one's eyes focused on the future was the key to a dynamic approach to life. When she was accused of having OCD, she took that as a badge of honor because to her mind it meant she was concerned about making sure things that had to get done, got done, even if it meant shouldering some anxiety and inconvenience.

Once again Sarah noticed that Robynn was conflicted, so she led her to an apple tree where a young man and a young woman sat holding hands. They said little and seemed satisfied to simply be next to each other. This too upset Robynn because the couple was not really accomplishing anything, not even planning the rest of their day. *Another waste of time!* This was Robynn's initial thought, but then she reconsidered because she began to feel a twinge of longing for this type of connection, a type of intimacy which she had foregone for the sake of completing one task after another.

Maybe being lost in the present moment is not a dysfunction, she began to think. *Maybe the present moment is of the essence of time, and I have passed over so many by looking ahead to get somewhere else. I've never even tried just being in the now. Is it possible that the purpose of time is to bask in it rather than run through it?*

Robynn looked at the little girl standing beside her holding on to one finger and singing a happy song that seemed to reverberate in Robynn's mind and then her heart. Never had she met anyone like this little girl or like that family or like the girl with her poetry or like the romantic couple beneath the tree. They seemed complete and tranquil. They were rooted in a joy that sprang, not from achievement, but from the wonder of the present. They seemed to bask in a perpetual now.

And it was at this point that Robynn's curiosity got the best of her. This was not the world she was familiar with, so what world was she in? Robynn knelt down on one knee, faced her little guide and asked the question that burned in her mind and heart, "Sweetheart, where am I?"

Sarah smiled a soft knowing smile and led Robynn to another hill which did not overlook the valley. As they ascended the hill, the scene became brighter and brighter until they reached the pinnacle. When Robynn stood at the top of the hill, it was as if she were looking straight into the sun. But she was not blinded nor burned. She felt that she could see better than ever before because she was in the presence of the source of all light. And she began to cry both from a sense of absolute relief from her worries and plans and because she seemed to understand in a new and blinding light what her life should really be all about. She looked down at the little girl and asked, "What do you call this place, Sarah?"

"It's heaven. It's where there is no movement of time, just a forever moment of joy and fullness."

"Have I been wrong to chase after so many things and devote myself to doing and having? Have I missed time by travelling so fast through it?"

"You have not been wrong," replied Sarah with a wisdom belied by her age. "You have just been distracted. Your world sees time as a commodity to use wisely and invest in thoughtfully. Younger people are fixated on the future; older people get lost in the past. And the present is forgotten. But life's truest values are in those moments of wonder and awe that you bask in without the feeling that they are fleeting. Human hearts are restless till they rest in the perpetual present. That's what heaven is. The end of time."

And as this thought came to Robynn, a heaviness settled upon her. She felt blood oozing down her face and neck. She felt the pressure from the car's crumbled roof on her rib cage as she struggled to breathe. Then she heard the bustle of movement just outside her car. The emergency squads had arrived and were frantically trying to evaluate the situation and save her from calamity. But the sounds were muffled, seemed far away. They kept receding more and more into the background. She tried desperately to check the chronometer on her free arm, but it was smashed and worthless. She did not know how long she had been in this situation, and she did not know how long she had left. Time seemed irrelevant.

Then, as her life blood drained out of her and the labor of breathing became too much to bear, Robynn, the efficiency expert, the master of the time continuum, the queen of getting things done, let go of her striving for what was not here yet, and let the moment overtake her. And in the blink of an eye she found peace in the everlasting now of heaven.

I've wasted so many moments in my life! How should I spend the time I've got left? Maybe being older is not about craving something else but about being thankful for the here and now.

Part II: Chapter Eleven

(JOURNAL ENTRY #11)

Journal #11

This will be my last journal entry. I'm scheduled to see Michael tomorrow, and I'm looking forward to it. I won't be adding anything with this entry, just reviewing and reconsidering some of my thoughts so I can remember all my questions and concerns at our session.

First off, my retirement. What am I supposed to do with it? Rocking chair retire or move on to new adventures? I'd hate to waste this time in my life, especially since my generation will probably be living the retired life longer than any previous generation. What should my retirement mean, since it's not like the kind of life I've been used to for so long?

Next, is it so horrible to grow old? What if I could become un-old, return to my youth? Would this be a good thing or not? I have gained a good deal of wisdom and knowledge in my seventy-three years. Doesn't that count for something? I surely don't want to return to high school!

Third, I know that as I age, I get closer to my death. What am I supposed to do with that? Even though I can't give myself life, I surely have some control over when and how I die, even if that only means religiously making healthy life choices. What should my approach to my own death be?

Fourth, getting older is inevitable. Peter Pan is a myth. I need to figure out how to age with dignity and grace. And I should be able to do that once I find out what the reason for getting older is. I'd hate to become one of those crotchety old guys. Should I be glad that I'm getting older even though there are some aches and pains involved?

And last, what is the best way for me to spend the time I have left? Getting older is a function of time, but time is not outside my control. What is the best way to spend the time I have till I have no more time? And, who knows? Maybe I'm in for another wild ride. I just want to be buckled up and ready for it.

Part III: Chapter One

(THE RETURN TO COUNSELING)

I made sure I was on time because this meeting with Michael was very important to me. I knew it would be a combination of discussion and lecture because, after all, Michael was also a college professor, and you know what they are like.

I politely knocked on the door of the office and was greeted with a friendly, "Come on in, Don." Clearly he was expecting me and appeared glad to see me.

I brought my journal but was nervous about sharing it with him. After all, these were my most personal thoughts, and they were first-draft efforts that could have used some editing to look good enough. *What would he think of my poor efforts? What would he think of me after he read my deepest thoughts?* I left them raw so he could see where I was really at. They dealt with important issues when it came to becoming a senior, but they were far from complete. I was a little embarrassed by them since they made me look like I didn't know what I was talking about even though I was living through them. I decided I was going to try to do the best I could with this situation, be as honest and genuine as I could be. I believed I could trust Michael, but I also believed he knew we all are flawed.

When I entered the room which was comfortably decorated with drapes, indirect lighting, a desk and two comfortable chairs already facing each other as they were the last time we met, I noted with delight that Michael had already brewed coffee for both of us. His hospitality was much appreciated. He was sitting in his chair looking at what appeared to be notes for our meeting. He had a hot cup of coffee on the lampstand next to him, a signature sign that he was serious about having a conversation with me. He had told me that he always had hot coffee ready when he did his counseling because his own experience of being counseled included sharing coffee with his mentor, Fr. David. He called the gesture of sharing a hot beverage with someone he was going to speak with, "common grounds of being here."

"May I pour you a cup of coffee, Don? I just brewed it a couple of minutes ago."

"Sure," I replied.

"I forget. Do you take cream and sugar?"

"Only a little bit of cream. Please no artificial stuff."

He put his notes aside and went over to the coffee pot. After he finished pouring the coffee and adding half-and-half, he handed the cup and saucer to me and we both sat down. He looked at me with a smile.

"Glad you could come today," he said warmly. "It's been a while. From your phone call it seems like you've been working hard on your concerns. I'm very interested in reading your journal, with your permission of course. You know, not everyone I work with takes journaling seriously. I hope it was of help to you."

I answered, "It was, Michael," then I took my first swig of coffee. "I believe putting my thoughts down led me to a deeper level of thinking. I could even imagine stories that dealt with the topics I was concerned with. My writing, my thinking, my imagining—it all helped me get in touch with where I was regarding my getting older. I was prompted to think 'outside my box' about the issues that were troubling me, and I found myself coming up with some tentative answers."

"I'm glad to hear that, Don. Did you bring your journal with you?"

"I did. But I'm a little nervous about letting you see it. It makes me uncomfortable whenever someone else is in on my secrets."

"That's understandable," he responded. "We're all afraid to bare ourselves before someone else. But if you can find someone whom you can trust and who can use your thoughts to help you resolve your issues, then the fear turns into amazement and joy. I just hope that I am such a person for you."

He kept looking me straight in my eyes and said, "I don't say that lightly because I myself went through a lot of pretty intense experiences with my doubts and conversion and all. It was because of my wife and because of Fr.

David who was my trusted mentor and friend that I got through it. When he died, I promised that I would take up his work and try to be a trusted mentor and friend to whomever would come to see me."

"I trust you, Michael. It's just hard to do this."

"I know, but hopefully together we can come to some insights that can help you see your way through to the rest of your life. You will continue to get older and aging will confront you more and more. It will become an obstacle for you until we wrestle with it and come to terms with it."

I realized that Michael was absolutely right. I'm fated to get older. But he had made a distinction between getting older and aging. That made me curious enough to do my best to control what reservations I had about letting him read my journal.

"Well, Michael, how do we begin?"

"First off," he replied, "I'll make you a trade." Then he reached over to his desk and picked up a paper-clipped stack of typed pages. "I did some homework too," he said as he handed his *A Reflection on Becoming Older* to me. "I'll take your journal home, read it and think about it. We'll talk about this unpublished article while we're here. How's that?"

I liked the way he suggested things rather than prescribed them. It made me feel like I was his collaborator rather than his student. So I gladly went along with his proposal, and we traded our manuscripts.

Michael then launched right into the discussion. "OK, now that that's done, let's talk about your growing old. I recall that the last time we talked, you spoke of a feeling of dread over getting older, like it meant a slow slide to deterioration and death. And that depressed you. You wanted to find out if that's what getting old is really all about, and what you can do about it. Is that a fair summary of what you told me last time?"

I was pleased that he had understood where I was coming from. So I said, "That's an accurate abridged version of my wandering thoughts on the subject. But now that I've been reflecting and journaling on getting older, I believe I have a better grasp on what it's all about. Still, I'm not sure if I have it right. That's why I need to talk to you."

Michael sat back in his chair and sipped his coffee. "Thank you for trusting that I might be helpful to you, Don. I hope I can live up to your expectations. So let's begin with you telling me what getting older now means to you, and especially why your thoughts about it have had such negativity about them."

I took a sip of coffee to bolster my courage and clear my head then I said, "When I see old pictures of myself, I can tell that things have changed with me. This becomes so very clear when I look over my photo albums and compare how I looked as a young father and how I look now as a grandfather. There's no denying that I have aged.

"You know, I heard you just now make a distinction between getting older and aging, but from what I see and what I feel, there's no difference. As I get older, I age, and by aging, I mean I lose what I had in my youth. My vibrant looks, my energy, my joy at living. Now I have hip and knee replacements, receding and greying hair, age spots, lapses in memory, possible glaucoma, less sexual power and so much less energy that I have trouble staying up past 9 pm. All of this makes me think of growing older as a lessening of my powers, a deterioration of my life leading inevitably to such constraints that my life becomes nothing more than a case of complete dependency and then death. When I think of getting older, I think of honey flowing down a blackboard. It starts out hell bent for leather, then it slows down, then it crusts up and stops. That's why I feel anxiety about getting older, Michael. It's because I fear it's really the crusting over of my life."

I stopped talking because I was getting choked up with emotion. I took another sip from my coffee cup, pulled myself together and finished up by saying, "And what really gets me is the suspicion that after all that I've undergone in my life, both the good and the bad parts, it all ends in my demise. Michael, if all of this leads only to death, then why go through it?

"You see, I sure as hell had fun in my younger days, but now I have aches and pains I never expected to have. If all these limitations and breakdowns are a natural part of living, then what's the living for? Just to suffer? Is getting older really a slow lapse into uselessness and misery? Is it the final proof that life is meaningless, and if so, wouldn't it have been better if I had died when I was younger?" I paused, then said, "I have to stop now, Michael, because I'm just getting worked up and confused."

Michael put down the notepad and pen he had in his hands and gazed at me with eyes that seemed so comforting and understanding. He said, "Don, you indeed have thought this through, and you know well how to share your thoughts and feelings. This is a big, big step in your getting a grip on your ideas and emotions. I think you have found a good place for us to start from.

"Of course we can't deal with everything you talked about today. So let's just try to see why you seem to have such a negative perspective on getting older and whether it's the best way to approach what you're going through."

I said, "I know our time is limited. But I hope in the time we do have we can get pretty far along."

"Good," he responded. "I'd like to begin by asking you what it means to mature."

"It means growing into a time when your body and mind have developed as much as they can."

"So an infant is not mature due to the fact that its limbs, its organs, and especially its brain are far less than they might be if allowed to develop as much as they can?"

"That's right," I noted.

"And although adolescents might look like starter-adults physically, they still don't have the mental or emotional capacity to adequately take on adult challenges or relationships."

I thought I knew where Michael was leading me, but I also knew he could go nowhere without me jumping in with him. So I followed his lead telling him, "I remember when I was in high school how I didn't have the physical strength nor the coordination to be good at sports. I had to wait till I was in college to be competitive. I also remember how I was so unsure of myself in high school that I readily went along with whatever group would accept me. Everything then was such a big deal emotionally. When my first girlfriend, Cindy, broke up with me, I was devastated and even considered calling it quits on life."

Michael moved his chair closer to me then pointed out, "Then I bet there came a time when you found you were able to handle projects and emotional crises that before seemed too daunting. Right?"

"Yep. Sounds like you've been there too."

"Have you ever noticed the difference in behavior between the 'party boy' who goes into the army and the responsible man who comes out? A similar change often occurs when young men become fathers. They take their responsibilities as fathers seriously and give up childish ways.

Wouldn't you say that with maturity comes skill and insights that were not available prior to reaching it?"

"Absolutely," I agreed.

"Now perhaps we should ask whether when we become adults the process of maturing comes to an end."

I was off-balance but answered, "I once thought that becoming an adult meant you were now at a kind of plateau in your life. There were challenges, yes, but no serious ups and downs like in adolescence."

"And what did you discover?"

"That being an adult doesn't mean you no longer have ups and downs. It means you now have ups and downs that challenge you at the adult level you're at."

"You're not the only one with that insight, Don. In fact there is a well-known psychologist named Erik Erikson who taught that each stage of human development has its own unique challenges. When a person meets these challenges, their reward is to graduate to a new stage of human development. And, guess what that means? The challenges never end. Growth and excellence as a human being depend on how we deal with these challenges at each stage of development. In a very real sense, we never finished maturing."

I was engrossed in what Michael was saying. So I listened intently. "Take growth plates," he continued. "At first, children's fingers are unfinished in terms of their length. As they get older these growth plates close when the fingers have grown to their capacity. We might say their fingers have matured. But maturity is not the end point for the fingers. Having matured, fingers have not reached the finish line of what they're all about. They have merely come to the point when, by the very fact of their maturity, they can develop skills and do things they could never have done before. Maturity is less their final condition than their readiness to do what fingers can possibly do.

"If you think about it, Don, getting older and maturing have a lot in common with the refinement of quality scotch and bourbon. These liquors get better with age because by maturing in various wooden barrels they attain a status of sophistication of fragrance and taste that only adding years can bring."

Michael looked poised to make the point he was driving at this whole time. "Don, you and I are adults, our overall growth plates have closed, but as is the case with fine liquors, that means that we have attained a type of sophistication in navigating life that we could never have had in our youth. We have, as it were, been aged in the barrel of life, not so that we can claim to be done with living, but so that living could be done at a new and higher level."

I moved closer to Michael in my chair because my interest and excitement over what Michael was alluding to grabbed my attention. "So you're saying, Michael, that growing old should not be confused with decline. Moving from infant to child, from child to adolescent, from adolescent to adult is in fact getting older but not a matter of personal decline. Rather, it's a matter of incline. But doesn't there come a point when a person has reached his or her optimal maturity and has no place to go but down?"

He answered with a knowing smile. "Maturity is fluid, Don. It never stops progressing unless we stop meeting the challenges facing us. I think being a senior citizen is just being at a different stage of maturity than what came before. It has its limitations, yes. It has its challenges, yes. But it's not necessarily marked by inevitable decline. Would you say that not being able to walk is a sign of decline for an infant? Is not being able to speak a sign of decline for a toddler? Is not being able to establish a stable, loving relationship a sign of decline for an adolescent? Not in the least. Rather they are signs of the limitations of a particular life stage and the call to progress to the next."

I felt confused, so I responded, "But my energy level is less than before. Isn't that a sign of decline?"

"Could be," replied Michael. "Yet don't you have the wisdom to complete tasks more efficiently with less energy. When you watch school children running and jumping and screaming at recess time, you might say they have a lot of energy, but you might also say it's wasted energy because it's uncontrolled and unfocused in the way you can use your energy. Wouldn't it be foolish to want to be like an elementary school child at recess? At your age you clearly don't need as much energy because you can conserve and focus your energy to get more things done than any wildly energetic child on a playground."

"Wow! That's a great way to look at it." I sat back and finally relaxed. "I think I'm beginning to see what you mean, Michael. I have certainly had a negative attitude toward getting older because I've been prejudiced toward youth. But isn't that attitude all around us in our culture? Look at advertisements on TV or in magazines. To be beautiful, you must look like a young person. To be strong, you must have the body of a 20-year-old. To be energetic, you've got to have youth on your side.

"But, as you say, at my age I have much more to offer the world around me now than I had when I was much younger. I can be beautiful and strong and energetic, but in a different way. And as I think about it, there were so many issues I was dealing with when I was younger that, looking back, I did not realize how naïve and ignorant I was then trying to confront them at that age before being ready to. They seem easy to resolve now with all my life experience. Maybe getting older is a growth in wisdom, not just a decline toward death."

Michael's slight smile told me he was pleased with my conclusions. He remarked, "I think now would be a good time to look at that article I gave you earlier. I have another copy right here that I can read along with you. If you don't mind, let's take a few minutes and silently look over what I have written and see if it dovetails with what we have been talking about."

"Sounds good, Michael. May I have a refill on my coffee?"

Michael took my cup, filled it, remembered the half-and-half, and handed it to me. We both fell silent as we read these words from Michael:

A Reflection on Becoming Older
by
Michael Balter

You may have heard some people in their 70's say that they have only a "few good years left." Why would someone speak this way? Why does the awareness of getting older prompt someone to make a statement that is so colored with shades of sadness and disappointment? Do athletes engage in a hard-fought competition with the thought that they have only a few more strokes or shots or plays left? Of course not, because if they did, they would undermine their own efforts with a defeatist attitude.

"Only a few good years left" should be banned from our thinking and speaking for many reasons. How can anyone speak with such confidence about the future? No one knows whether anyone has "few" or "many" years left to live. To say "few" is to express a rather pessimistic attitude toward a person's life development. Who can tell when they will experience deterioration or even death? It is clearly possible that a 75-year-old will live longer and better than a 25-year-old depending on personal behavior, personal habits and the unique circumstances of each person's life. And to couple the notion of "a few good years" with the notion of "only" intensifies a sentiment of gloom and inevitability. Those words are code for "I believe I am coming to the end of my life, and it will have diminishing value."

Understanding the process of advancing in years in terms of "only a few good years" is really expressing a sentiment of despair at being fated to a bad outcome to one's life. It is an attitude toward getting older that can be translated into this notion: "Shortly my life will be more of a burden than an opportunity because I will inevitably deteriorate to a state where life will not be worth living any longer." Or there is the oft-heard phrase, "It's all downhill from here." What could be more depressing than that? And what's more, thinking like this can easily become a self-fulfilling prophecy as a person simply gives up trying to live a healthy, happy life since it will soon come crashing down no matter how hard one tries.

This is an unhealthy approach to getting older as well as life in general. I believe there can be a more positive attitude toward advancing in years. It is a recognition of the inevitability of change but not a presumption of the inevitability of deterioration. Change can also bring about growth. All growth is itself a deterioration of one life stage and the emergence of a new one. For example, no one is sad when a baby emerges from the womb because this passage is not just the loss of one condition but the gaining of a new condition with greater possibilities. And no one is sad over a child's losing his or her baby teeth because the loss of these teeth is not a deterioration but a necessary step in the emergence of adult teeth. Likewise the loss of unwanted fat is not a sign of deterioration but of a healthier way of life. So the diminishment of one stage of life does not necessarily mean a worse life to come. What if a person were to refer to getting older in terms of the transition to a new form of living rather than the diminishment of an old form? For example, what if the decrease of natural collagen in one's face at 75 is not considered a deterioration of facial beauty but a new form of it?

Getting older can mean movement toward a different and perhaps better way of living. Certainly as a person gets older, aspects of a person often do not lend themselves to behaviors a person once performed. Older people often tire more easily than younger people and older people may not heal from injuries as fast as younger people do. But why would these facts lead to a pessimistic attitude? The fact is that change has occurred, not that evil has befallen. Being *different* does not mean *being worse than*. If a person sees being 70+ as just another stage of his or her life development, then that person will not see "being older" as a deterioration but as another situation which requires appropriate life adjustments.

It seems the biggest complaint about being older is that the person cannot do what he or she did earlier in life. But why would this cause concern in the first place? Infants can put their toes into their mouths, but when most people are older they can't do that, and this is no cause for sadness. Being older is a sign that the person has matured and is at another level of development, not that his or her overall capacities have diminished.

Likewise, experiencing "senior citizen" status is not by its very nature an experience of standing before a dark pit of inevitable destruction. It is experiencing a particular set of challenges, limitations and strengths that are appropriate for this stage of life and no other. Sometimes an elderly person "prefers" to be able to do what that person did at an earlier stage of life, but holding on to such preferences is not a mark of seeing how bad things are now but a sign that the elderly person cannot accept his or her current stage of life because a previous stage somehow seems better. No developmental stage of life is better than any other. Each stage holds a unique constellation of challenges and a unique set of talents and strengths that have been earned by losing hold of an earlier developmental stage. Holding on to such preferences for qualities of an earlier stage often leads to a sour attitude toward an elderly lifestyle. Because one cannot do what one once did does not mean that one cannot do something else, and this something else may be of superior quality. To see the loss of characteristics that refer to a previous life stage as an indication of diminishment of life and a march toward inability, insignificance and death is a grievous misunderstanding of a developmental stage. Moreover, it can lead to a lack of appreciation of the values and possibilities of the current stage, which in turn can lead to a giving up in the face of what appears to be a dismal and dreadful future.

Yes, the reality is that a 75-year-old cannot do some things a 25-year-old can, but likewise there are many things a 75-year-old can do that the 25-year-old cannot. Being 75 should not be treated as the diminished life of a 25-year-old but as the possibility of a full life as a 75-year-old. At 70+, life itself is not diminished. What is diminished is one's capacity to live as one did decades ago!

Being elderly requires different life strategies than were required at an earlier stage of life. These challenges cannot be met by a 25-year-old. It takes the experience, skills and wisdom developed over a lifetime to navigate the condition of being elderly. The challenges a senior citizen faces are not for the faint of heart. An older person is more likely to successfully meet these challenges than a younger one, because the older person has acquired the necessary experience, skills and wisdom that are simply not available to a younger person. Being 75 is not being less than 25. In fact, being a 25-year-old is being less than being a 75-year-old because the older person can say "been there, done that" about being 25 or 35 or 45... A 75-year-old is not limited to the experiences of a younger person but can engage a whole new set of challenges, possibilities and achievements. Being elderly is having the privilege to face one's life with a grace and confidence like never before.

Now, returning to the opening statement, it needs to be recognized that the quantity of a person's days is not as important as the quality of those days. So the number of days left to a 75-year-old is actually irrelevant. Not only can a 75-year-old outlive a 25-year-old, but the life of a 75-year-old can conceivably be fuller and richer and more satisfying.

What is important is the way one engages life and makes the most out of what one is given. A 70+-year-old needs be a shapeshifter and accommodate the unique character of being elderly rather than long for what life was at a younger age. Being a senior citizen should be approached as a new way of life, not the diminishment of an earlier stage of life. Being 75 can be wildly exciting, just as being 25 can be wildly exciting for a 25-year-old. In fact, being 70+ is often preferable to being in one's 20's because many responsibilities that were emotionally and physically taxing are now gone and life can be engaged in with a more reflective manner conducive to serenity and the actualization of dreams and hopes that were restricted by being at a previous life stage.

Getting older does not necessarily mean "going downhill." Rather it means living in a new way with new opportunities. What gets in the way is one's attitude toward getting older. If you approach it as a diminishment of life and a deterioration till death, that's how it will seem to you. You will create a self-fulfilling prophecy. But if you see being elderly as the next best way of being me, then life becomes as promising and engaging as it was when you were younger, only in a new way. Instead of bemoaning the process of advancing in age, perhaps a person should approach it thinking, "Look at all the life I've led. Look at all I am bringing to the life I have yet to lead." With this positive attitude, diminishment does not take center stage. This appreciation of getting older leads to encouragement and a search for joy in life, for the best is yet to be.

When I finished reading, I looked up at the clock on the wall and realized that the session was about to end. I then looked at Michael who was scribbling something on his notepad.

"I'm done, Michael."

Michael looked up and said, "Good. So what do you think?"

I was a little taken aback thinking that Michael would be the first to make sense of what we read since he was the author. But I recovered and with a bit of hesitation pointed out, "That was quite a read. I did relate a lot of it to what we were talking about. But since we don't have much time left in this session, let me just mention that it did make one point that I found very helpful. That the negative side of getting older may be more a matter of attitude than fact. I'm not like my 13-year-old granddaughter, and I don't want to be like her. Being younger is not all it's cracked up to be. Been there. Done that. Don't want to go through it again, especially pimples erupting and my voice cracking. I don't want to establish myself in a career. I don't want to search for a lifemate. I don't want to worry about whether I can take care of my family anymore. It's not that I hated my life when I was going through these things. I suppose, if I had to, I would do what I had to do over again. But I don't prefer it. I enjoyed being a father, but now that my children are grown and gone, I have moved on but cherish the memories.

"And, Michael, I guess that's what getting older is really all about, moving on to something else. But what else? If I'm to deal with becoming an elder as a 'moving-on,' then I surely would like to know what I'm moving on to. That's at the heart of my negative thoughts and feelings about advanced age. What is getting older for? For death? For a continuation of this life? For a moving on to another life? Can we talk about that next time, Michael?"

Michael looked me straight in the eyes and smiled. "I believe you have scored a bullseye with your request, Don. I hope you'll look over my article again as I'll read over and reflect on your journal entries. And we will do so with the question of the purpose of advancing in age front and center in our minds and hearts. You know it took me a good deal of time to find my purpose in life, and I must say you are part of it. And for that I thank you.

"So, Don, the next time we'll pursue the question of the purpose of getting older. Thanks so much for coming in. See you then."

We both stood up and I said, "Thank you, Michael." Then I turned and left the room feeling like my burden had been lightened and my heart enlightened not only by what we talked about but by the sincerity and kindness of a person who was unafraid to share himself with me. And that got me to thinking--could I have related with Michael as I did if I were a lot younger? "No" was the resounding answer. So maybe, just maybe, being older does not mean being less.

Part III: Chapter Two

(DON'S DREAM)

The night before I was to have my next meeting with Michael, I had a dream about a little boy and his mother sitting at the dining room table after the boy gets home from school. He loved this time because he could spend uninterrupted time with his mother, and because his mother always had milk and cookies waiting for him when he came home.

"Is it OK if I dunk my cookies, Mommy?" asked the little boy in anticipation of one of his favorite pastimes.

"It's quite alright now, but don't do it when your father's at the table. You know how he is about proper manners," answered his mother so happy that they had a close and honest relationship.

The boy stuffed a chocolate chip cookie dripping with milk into his mouth and tried to speak, but his mother warned him, "If you try to speak with your mouth full, you might choke. So chew your food before you try to say anything else to me."

He swallowed the rest of the cookie and then asked, "Who do you love best, Mommy? Daddy or me?"

This was the kind of question loving mothers try to avoid. They want their children to believe they are precious to them no matter what. Yet they need somehow to make clear that although their love is shared, it is not diminished. So the mother searched intently for an answer, then said, "I love you both as much as I can love, but I love you both in different ways. Let me explain.

"You're my treasure that makes my day brighter and my heart dance. You are my number one little person who I know will some day be a big person like

Daddy. I promise to take care of you and never leave you, no matter what. I try so hard to help you grow up big and strong, and I'm so proud of who you are. You do well at school. You study hard and you do your chores without complaining. You get along with the other kids in the neighborhood. How you keep your room is another story, but nobody's perfect."

The little boy laughed at this remark and then stuffed another milk-soaked cookie into his mouth. When his mouth was empty, he asked, "So how much do you love Daddy?"

The mother chose her words carefully, not wanting her son to think that she loved him any less because she loved his father with all her heart. Looking at the little boy who was becoming a cookie mess, the mother said, "I love Daddy like my best friend in the whole wide world. I have promised to always take care of him, and he has promised to always take care of me. I don't have to help him grow straight and strong. He's already straight and strong, and I know I can count on him to be there for me and for you no matter what. You will grow up and move away but Daddy will be here by my side for a long, long time. I'm so proud of what he has done, and I love him with all my heart."

And as soon as she uttered those last few words, she knew her son was disheartened because he asked, "How can you love Daddy with all your heart and have any love left over for me?"

She hesitated and thought about her answer carefully before she spoke. But before she could say anything more, the little boy said, "But Daddy's old and I'm young. He wears glasses and sometimes says his back and shoulders hurt. I can do a lot he can't do. Doesn't that count for something?"

It was the time of truth and honesty. But how does one explain that love is not diminished when it is shared? It actually burns brighter. She paused, then spoke from her heart. "Sweetheart, just like you can do things your Daddy can't because your younger, he can do a lot of things you can't because he's older. I love both of you differently, but not any less because you're different kinds of people. Love is a special thing. It's not like that cookie your holding that's just about to drop off into your milk. If you give me a piece of that cookie, there is less for you to eat. But if I love you as much as I can, that means I can love your daddy as much as I can, because love grows when it is shared. I never want to lose my cookie beast because you are part of me forever, and I never want to lose the love of my life because Daddy is a part of me forever. You are my <u>son</u> (she pointed at the boy), and Daddy, he is my <u>sun</u> (she pointed upwards)."

"*That's funny, Mommy, how you say that. So would you say that you would really like me to grow up to be like Daddy?*"

The mother's heart began to melt. "Sweetheart, I want you to grow up like the special person you are. I have two men in my life. My little man and my big man. You're being younger doesn't make you better than him, and his being older does not make him better than you. You both are priceless treasures to me, but in different ways. Always will be."

She smiled a loving smile at the little boy and wiped the chocolate moustache off his face with a napkin. Then she said, "I'm just a lucky lady to have such jewels in my life. Now give me a kiss and take you books to your room. You have about an hour to play outside before your father comes home and we have supper."

When I awoke from the dream I sat up in bed and resolved to never again demean myself because of my age. I may be different but I'm still me, and I'm still a treasure. I have a lot to offer, even if it hurts a little more when I offer it.

Part III: Chapter Three

(THE FINAL
COUNSELING SESSION)

I was getting ready to leave my house to meet with Michael again when I thought, *it's really been something, going through all this stuff about getting older. I think I'm staving off dementia just by working through all the things I've come up with, plus all the things I've gained from Michael. I'm not as anxious or depressed about what it means to get older anymore. Maybe it's true that knowledge is power. When you know what you're facing, you somehow can handle it. If it remains mysterious, it seems to handle you.*

I'm beginning to understand that distinction between getting older and aging Michael made at the last session. Being older has to do with accumulating more years under my belt. Aging is more about how I am when I'm older. Even young people age when they are overwhelmed with difficulties or if they turn to drugs to help them through the rough patches. And I've met some people who don't seem to age even though they're older. Likewise I've met people that simply "do not act their age" which implies that adding years should include an advance in wisdom and grace but sometimes doesn't. Aging refers to the way I live my life, not the number of years I've lived. If I live poorly and am on the way to disability and death, I age. If I approach being older in terms of fresh opportunities for growth, then I can recapture the lust for life I had in my earlier years, and I fend off aging. It's these fresh opportunities that I need to talk to Michael about. How does a person add years to their life in a healthy and happy way? What's the secret to having a meaningful and exhilarating life even though you might be a senior citizen? I'm beginning to think a big part of the experience of getting older is my own attitude towards it. So maybe I should have an "attitude adjustment" with regard to being in my 70's. Develop a more positive approach to it.

Maybe I shouldn't try to make getting older go away. Maybe I should embrace advancing in years and find out what good can come from it. Is getting older a curse or an opportunity? Before I met with Michael, I was afraid of being older because I had the feeling that it was a curse. Since I've been talking with him, I'm not so sure it's such a bad thing. But I still need to be clear about how it can be a good thing.

What if advancing in years was a natural benefit to me, something I should actually be thankful for and embrace? Then I would be concerned, not with avoiding it, but with doing it well. But what exactly is the goal of my getting older? I would be willing to give myself to advancing in years if I knew what it leads to, and whether whatever that may be is worth the effort to attain it.

I had to stop thinking because time was moving on and I didn't want to be late for my session with Michael. So I finished dressing and drove to Michael's office. As I was in the car, I felt a kind of giddiness, because I was anticipating some resolution to the issues that had been swirling around in my head for so long.

I arrived, parked the car and walked up to the second floor where Michael had his office. It was not really Michael's office but the area where Michael had his office. It was something like a cooperative venture with several mental health professionals sharing the same space, each having a private office off the main reception area.

This arrangement suited Michael well because his being a counselor was Michael's second job. He was a fulltime philosophy professor at the university, but he made himself available to people like me. From what I could gather, most of Michael's clients were like me, people who were confused and searching for ways out of personal dilemmas like facing their advancing years or like failing at one thing or another or like just being confused about what their lives are all about. That's why I was feeling a sense of gratitude for his meeting with me. He could be spending his time with so many others, but he chose to spend it with me. Which reminded me of the dream I had last night. I figured that even though I was a senior, I must be precious in his sight.

I knocked on Michael's door, and when he opened it, he greeted me with a warm, "Welcome, Don. I'm glad you're here. Come on in. Coffee?"

"Of course," I responded. "It's what greases the wheels of our conversation."

Michael shut the door, invited me to sit down in the same chair I sat in last time, and brought me a cup of steaming coffee prepared the way I like it. *He remembered!* Michael sat down across from me, took a sip of his coffee and began to speak.

"Don, I read over your journal entries last night. Very impressive, I must say. They are honest, insightful and genuine. Not everyone takes this assignment as seriously as you have.

"I found that there is a clear progression in your writing which indicates that you've been moving naturally through a process of insight and decision. Please keep in mind that I can only assist you with that movement, Don. My role is not to take your place in the process of dealing with what has been bothering you. I can only offer suggestions that hopefully help you to resolve your issues for yourself. It's a joint effort, yes, but, ultimately, it's up to you what you do with it. Your coming here and your producing this journal shows me that you're well along the way of finding peace in your passion. Here's your writing back because I bet you want to continue your exceptional work." Michael handed my journal to me, but I felt like he was handing me some kind of diploma.

Then he said, "Well, I think from your writing and our last conversation that what we need to confront today is the purpose of getting older. Am I right?"

I felt very relaxed and confident, so I quickly replied, "Yes. You're spot on. I'm beginning to have a picture of being a senior citizen that is more positive than ever before. I used to believe that growing older was only growing closer to death. As I grew older I became less until I faded from life all together. But now I can see that being advanced in years may be just another stage along life's way. It may in fact be a second adolescence because at my age I'm revisiting so many of the questions and challenges I faced when I was in my teenage years--Who am I? What's life all about? Where is all this going?"

Michael smiled and said, "Funny you should say that, Don, because that's what Erickson says is the hallmark of old age, the consideration of what my life has meant and whether it's been worth it. A healthy person at your age naturally becomes a philosopher to sort out the meaning of what they have been through and where they're yet going."

"So maybe I should switch from being your client to being your student?"

Michael chuckled. "You would be more than welcome, but formal education in philosophy is not a requirement. What is necessary is thinking through where you are right now and what it's for. It's not easy, but it's worth it."

"So what now?" I asked.

"What would you think about our focusing our attention on whether there even is any purpose to getting older?"

My interest was piqued because we were finally getting to the meat of the problem. "Michael, if I only knew why I'm getting older and whether there is some good reason for becoming an elder, I think I could control my negative thoughts and feelings and maybe even set up a good plan for the rest of my life."

"Great!" said Michael. "Can I top off your coffee?" Michael stood up and reached over to get my cup. I handed it to him with a hearty, "Thanks."

As he handed me my refilled cup and then sat down, he asked, "So do you think that getting older might actually have a purpose, and if so, what might that be?"

It was a crucial question that caught me off guard since I was expecting him to enlighten me. Now I was on the hook to start the conversation. I knew what he was trying to do. Get me to work through this myself rather than be passive and dependent on him. I picked up my cup, took a long sip from it, set it down and tried to get our dialogue on the right foot.

I began with some hesitation stating, "First off, moving on in years is inevitable. But people experience what you referred to as 'aging' in different ways and at different times in their lives. Aging sometimes comes on people because of poor lifestyles or traumatic events. I've seen people in their 30's and 40's who look like they're my age. My getting older is a matter of time, not necessarily a matter of aging.

"It's like what happens to a pair of tennis shoes. They're clean and stiff at first, then when they're broken in, they work just fine. But with time and use they begin to wear out. That's my type of getting older, Michael. I guess I'm just wearing out. But isn't that the way of all things in this world? Doesn't everything wear out?"

Michael joined in enthusiastically. "I fully understand what you're talking about. Philosophers and poets and playwrights have all emphasized how fleeting life is. My dad was fond of kinda quoting Shakespeare by saying in a most dramatic fashion, 'we are all poor players who strut and fret our time upon the stage and are heard no more.' Seems rather pessimistic and fatalistic if you ask me, but it does speak to the fleeting character of our lives."

I picked up the thread immediately. "If we wear out, then we have a deadline to our lives."

"Plato thought that life was in fact a preparation for death."

"And that's what scares me, Michael. If my death is inevitable, does it mean that my life is all in vain? Do I have nothing to look forward to other than being a feast for worms?"

"You put it so delicately, Don," Michael remarked, and we both laughed.

Then I continued, now more engaged than ever. "Maybe that's where the negativity comes from in my thinking about getting older. I wear out, I die and that's it? So wouldn't it be better to choose a time and place for my own death rather than rust away with age till I simply can't move any longer?"

Michael took on a serious tone. "I've had personal experience with a close friend trying to commit suicide. It's not pretty. But for some it probably would seem a better alternative than staying around living if all you have to look forward to is falling apart and toppling over."

I joined in saying, "Sometimes I imagine myself stuck in a wheelchair in a nursing home where I'm abandoned by my children and friends as well as by the nursing home staff. One day I call out 'Take me home,' and no one pays any attention. Then I give up and give out. They only notice me when they find me slumped over in my wheelchair with the pallor of death surrounding me."

"You certainly can come up with some vivid images, my Friend."

Seeing Michael so attentive, I charged on saying, "That's where that negativity comes in. The thought that advancing in years ends up with death as a whimper. If that's all I have to look forward to at my age, it's really depressing."

Michael enthusiastically responded, "I think you have hit on something very important, Don, and it has to do with the question--what do you have to look forward to at your age? It seems to me that if all you have to look forward to is dying, there really is no purpose to getting older, because then it's nothing more than a process of decline and demise. So maybe we should pursue the question whether we can find a natural purpose for advancing in years, a purpose that encourages a person to look forward to living and maybe even to something beyond death."

"I'm game. How should we do this?"

He changed course for a moment saying, "Just to let you know, this may take a little while longer than the allotted time for this session. I would like to pursue this with you anyway, if that's OK with you. I won't charge you extra."

I responded in a light-hearted way, "Well, if that's the case, how can I look a gift horse in the mouth? Let's do it."

"OK. Let's start with the fact that our lives are fleeting, like everything else in our universe. Philosophers call this aspect of the world *finitude*, the fact that nothing in our world lasts forever. So then what is the meaning of this universal characteristic?"

"That nothing really matters?"

"I would rather say that nothing remains. Everything has a limit to its existence. Plants and animals live a limited life but are not aware of being limited. They exist and one day just cease to exist. In other words when their time is up, they just drop dead and decay into humus. But inhabitants of this universe like you and me, we are aware that we do not remain forever in this world, and therefore we are faced with figuring out what 'being fleeting' means for the way we live.

"For one thing, Don, having a natural deadline to our lives means we must act. We can't leave things till tomorrow. Procrastination is unnatural, although common. Knowing we will die is the motivation to do and have and be before it's too late. So the 'fleeting' character of our lives makes life a series of opportunities and projects rather than a plateau of apathy."

I was really intrigued by this train of thought because it seemed we were finally coming upon the answer I was seeking. I sat forward in my chair and asked, "But what is it we are doing and having and being for? What is getting older meant for? How could it be a platform of opportunity?"

"You really are testing the waters here, Don," replied Michael. "But a resolution to this whole issue of getting older and being elderly may be on the horizon. Let's consider this--if you had to characterize infancy and childhood in a single word what would you say?"

I sat back in my chair and answered confidently, "Dependency. Infants are helpless without care from others. And toddlers may make forays into walking and talking, but they rely on others to guide them to do these things."

"And what about older children?"

"They are dependent but not helpless. Every parent faces the challenges that comes with the 'willfulness' of children as they come into their own. So if I had to choose a single word to characterize this next stage of development I would say 'self-centered.' That's because although they might happily interact with relatives and friends, their goal is to meet their own needs so they can succeed in the world around them."

"And adolescents?"

I let out a laugh and pronounced, "Since they are really older children, I would say definitely 'self-centered,' maybe even 'self-indulgent.' In my many years as a high school history teacher I experienced one student after another struggling to find their own identity and to get a realistic hold on their newfound urges, especially when it comes to sex. Even though many of my students were involved in service activities, they still seemed to be motivated by filling their needs for self-sufficiency, approval and a personal sense of destiny."

Michael chuckled as he asked, "Are you sure you're not a psychology teacher?"

"Actually, that was my college minor, and I sometimes taught Psych 101 along with my history classes."

I was now feeling good about myself since Michael's question clearly showed appreciation for my standing in the discussion. With renewed assurance I took charge of the dialogue posing the question, "And what about adults? Michael, how would you characterize their approach to living?"

Michael had no trouble taking on the role of respondent. "I would say they are more integrated and skilled adolescents."

"What do you mean by that?" My facial expression must have signaled confusion and doubt because Michael moved forward in his chair both to explain and to defend his idea.

"What I mean is that adults have developed the wherewithal to navigate the challenges of life regarding basic survival, social interaction, goal-setting and achievement. Yet adults display an underlying attitude of self-centeredness as well. Take for example the typical employee, whether professional, skilled or unskilled. Why are they active in employment?"

I didn't know whether Michael's question was rhetorical or aimed at me. I jumped in with an answer anyway. "For the benefits. The money, the career advancement, the reputation. And come to think of it, it seems that the care they show their families and the community is tinged with the sense that they are demonstrating care in order to get it back for themselves."

Michael then blended his thoughts with mine. "There is no question that adults, like myself, can display caring and can get a lot of joy from their work, but if you ask most any adult why they become involved in this or that, they would admit if they were honest that it comes down to what they can get out of it. Adults in general live in a doing and getting and having world. Even when they're on vacation or just relaxing around the house, they are asking themselves whether it's worth it to engage in these things so long as they're beneficial to them."

I interjected, "But that underlying purpose is so universal and deep it seems both natural and necessary."

"And so it is," responded Michael. "You can't achieve anything in life without it. And if being an adult is about anything, it's about achieving things like health and security and contentment. Without this 'underlying purpose' as you call it, it would be hard to see how anyone could avoid the pitfalls of living and attain to any real success in life."

I was confused. "So is there a problem here? It seems to me that this self-centeredness is not only a universal trait of human adults but a necessary one for attaining a good life."

It was clear that Michael was basking in this give-and-take. This was his universe of discourse and he was bent on pursuing it as far as we could. "Here is the problem. Like so many things in life, Don even this basic orientation of adults gets skewed and twisted until it results in adults setting up obstacles rather than pathways for their own happiness."

"How so?"

"By concentrating on accumulation. The quantity and quality of material goods, the superiority of reputation, the eminence of one's power over things and people. A person's life makes sense in terms of winning and losing a game. More and better stuff equals a sign of winning. Better and greater reputation equals being successful. Lording it over others means being a superior person. The temptation for this approach is so overwhelming that most everyone indulges in it from time to time. Myself included. I have to work hard at curbing my tendency to be proud of my power to influence others as a teacher and counselor. It's so easy to think that I'm superior to my students and clients because of what psychologists call the 'power differential' that I wield. And this arrogance is a real threat to mutual respect and dialogue because it destroys honesty and replaces it with one-up-man-ship."

"But I don't feel you're trying to dominate me."

"I'm very thankful for that, because domination by either a counselor or a client is the death of healthy and healing dialogue."

Michael hesitated, then went on to say, "Well, this conversation is not about me, but is really about what getting older is meant for. And it seems we have veered off course with our characterizations of different stages of human life. But in fact it was all necessary to get to your stage of life."

"And, pray tell, what is that?" I asked.

"It's the point of adulthood when the self-centered purposes that previously served you well no longer gear with your sense of yourself. Which is precisely why you feel lost and confused. You are no longer meant for the doing and getting and having mode of regular adulthood."

I was totally engaged at this point and posed the question, "What *am* I meant for then at my age?"

"I think maybe you should answer that question yourself since it's where you're at."

I felt resentment and anger at that comment. I thought, *If I knew the answer to that, I wouldn't need to come to you, Michael!* Yet I could tell by his concerned look that Michael was sympathizing with my negative feelings over his turning the spotlight back on me. *He knows I've been trying but not getting it. Why does he think I can do it now? Yet he's been kind to me throughout these sessions and has supported me so I could come to insights that were genuinely mine, not borrowed from him. I think that's what he's doing now.*

So even though I felt off balance and ill-prepared, I gave a tentative response. "This is hard, Michael, but maybe it's necessary for me to do myself since it's my life, after all. Well, what I'm gathering from our discussion so far is that we naturally go through various stages in our lives. That is, of course, if we are healthy. If health is missing, I can see how we can regress and maybe even get stuck in earlier stages. But I'm healthy. My aches and pains and the age-related limitations to my abilities do not make me overall unhealthy. I still can get around and think and laugh. It's just I need to adjust how I do those things given my conditions."

I stopped talking and sat silently for a moment. I reached over and sipped my coffee to fill the void. But it was not a void; it was a dawning of insight. I just couldn't articulate it yet. So I had to take some time before I spoke again. Michael said nothing. He just waited silently yet attentively as if to let me know it was OK to get ready and that he would be there when I returned to the conversation. Then it came to me and I surprised myself with what I said.

"Michael, I've got enough stuff. I've already earned respect as a teacher. I've known love, although to this day I miss my Joannie. I keep contact with my son and my daughter and enjoy being with my grandchildren. My house is paid for, my car is fully mine, my bank account is solid, and my pension and social security incomes are both steady and sufficient. There is nothing more I must have and there is nothing more I have to do to get anything I can't live without. So the prime tasks of typical adulthood are no longer on my shoulders. I'm past that. But I don't feel like I'm finished with my life. What is it that I'm missing, Michael? Maybe you could step in right now."

Michael looked grateful and fascinated by my ideas. He took up the reins of the discussion saying, "Perhaps it all gets back to your notion of 'wearing out.' What has worn out for you is not your body nor your mind but the lifestyle you've maintained all your adult life so far. You have succeeded in life by focusing on doing and getting and having. Now you're experiencing a premonition of your death, not necessarily so much because you're slipping toward physical demise, but because you're experiencing the need for your old lifestyle to fade away. Your well-worn approach to your life has become outmoded. After all this time you have finally reached a point where you no longer need to live as if everything ultimately was about you and about your welfare. Maybe attaining your age is not really a 'wearing out' but a 'ripening,' a being ready to live your life in a new way. Maybe reaching your seniority is not really about recreation as much as it is about re-creation, the dawning of a new personal maturity."

"How could this be, Michael?"

Michael seemed elated to share what obviously were truths near and dear to his heart. He spoke as if he were sharing a profound yet practical secret to life. He said, "As you yourself pointed out, we human beings begin as fully dependent, then we move on to a lifestyle marked by self-centeredness as we try to get everything we can get out of life. And this would be sufficient and fulfilling for human beings if all that a human being happened to be about is surviving.

"But, Don, have you noticed that as you have matured through adulthood you have less need to think about your own welfare and tend more to concern yourself about what is not you. Take becoming a parent. How often I have noticed a remarkable change in the attitude of people toward themselves and the world around them when they become parents. They almost magically change from self-centered egoists to dutiful and self-sacrificing caregivers. Having children naturally changes a person's focus from self to other. We learn to subordinate ourselves to the needs of others and we embrace inconvenience to serve rather than to siphon off what is good. As I see it, personal maturity is a natural but slow process of focusing your attention away from yourself, of no longer considering yourself the center of the universe."

Michael stopped, drank some coffee then plunged on. "Don, the point I'm getting at is maybe you have ripened in your progress toward full maturity. Maybe you now are ready to throw off the old self that is really all about itself and take on a new self that's no longer concerned with doing and getting and having what you need. Maybe you're at a point where you need to focus away from yourself and share your personal abundance. Maybe being a senior is not just about reaping what you have sown, but it's about discovering and engaging new dimensions that go beyond yourself that foster a higher level of being for you and whatever you touch."

"That's a lot to take in, Michael. You make being a senior sound like having a grand opportunity to project yourself beyond yourself into new and bold adventures. You seem to think that being a senior is an opportunity to do just that, not to get something out of it, but because it's the next step of maturity which is fulfilling and exciting in itself."

"Don, I believe it's the same adventure that colors all our life stages but which we lose sight of because we are distracted by so much doing and getting and having. It does get our attention in times of crisis but then fades when things go back to normal. It gets our attention during adolescence because we are intently focused on who we are and the purpose of our lives. Then we get into a routine of doing and getting and having where we lose sight of what we attended to with our coming of age.

"But what follows, if all goes well, is a time when, like you, we come to a stage of ripeness when questions of life's meaning and our role in it stand front and center once again. But this time the habits of doing and getting and having no longer need to be front and center. What springs up is a freedom to explode out with the joy of living as much as possible. To step onto the stage of the world and show who you are and what you can give yourself to, fearlessly taking on whatever comes next. And that includes death as maybe a doorway to what's beyond the boundaries of this world."

"Do you believe in an afterlife? Michael."

"I do, Don. I do because I believe there is a God who created and sustains everything in this world. And I do because I believe that God is accessible to me and has promised that if I identify with Him and am faithful to his commands, I will live with Him in permanent joy. I see the fleeting nature of this world in stark contrast to this afterlife of unending happiness. For me, the purpose of the world's impermanence is to prompt us to long for and work toward the permanence of heaven which is everlasting because God is everlasting.

"You know, Don, I've thought about this afterlife thing deeply and for a long time. I have experienced some things I wish I had never experienced, but through it all I have come to find the purpose of my life to be to share the Spirit of Love in any way I can. I'm still moving along life's way as an adult because I can't just bask in the wonder of teaching and counseling. I'm still required to approach them as means to taking care of my Emilee, my son, Davey, and myself so we don't sink under the adversities of this world. But someday I look forward to living like you can, Don, free of all the things that encumber the pure joy of living and loving."

Michael took a deep breath and continued, "Now, I know this pure joy is hard if not impossible to come by here in this world, even when you can be free from doing and getting and having as you are. But you have a splendid opportunity at your age to live just such a life."

Michael spoke with glassy eyes and soft words. "So, as you can see, I'm jealous of you because you're at a point in your life when life can be about joy rather than survival. For me advancing in years is the process of coming to full maturity, of being detached from whatever distracts you from appreciating and reverencing and taking care of things for the pure joy of it. Because you now don't have to get something out of what you do, what you do can come to pass as pure love, a devotion to the goodness of everyone and everything motivated by nothing else than pure care and joy in engagement. Getting older, Don, is meant to free you up to live a life of devotion and joy.

"And, Don, even if you don't share my faith, you will find that living out of pure love brings such peace and joy that you will find your life to be worthwhile all the way to its end."

I sat back in my seat amazed by Michael's inspiring words. But, come to think of it, they did not originate just from Michael. He was sharing what we together had come to. He just added his personal perspective on it. I was now somehow free of worry and overcome with a sense of happiness and excitement. But I had to get come clarity on one more thing. So I asked, "In practical terms what does this new perspective on life involve?"

Michael seemed spent after sharing his insights, but he soldiered on apparently because of what I needed. "Great question, Don, and again I will throw it back to you. Can you think of activities you could get involved in that are more about being joyful than being useful?"

I thought for a while then replied, "I'm afraid that up till now I've been driven by ulterior motives. But you are talking about living without ulterior motives. Living to appreciate the moment, the people, the things around me, even myself if for no other reason than to bask in their beauty and goodness. Sounds like a life of mindfulness and meditation."

Michael perked up and said, "Don, you have reached a point in your life where you can be who you are and touch whatever you choose to share yourself with, without thinking of yourself. You are primed to act selflessly. I call this self-transcendence. Having fulfilled all your needs for survival and safety and personal relationship and self-confidence, you now are free and empowered to shower the world and all that is in it with a creative spark, like at the outset of creation. You are ripe for a life meant for creating a better world of beauty and love."

I caught his meaning and blurted out, "I get it now! Becoming elderly is for being self-transcendent. And being self-transcendent means to be like God—to love for no ulterior motive and to create so that everything can prosper. And being like God conquers death so you can live in unending freedom and joy."

Michael rocked back and forth in his chair as he clapped his hands and laughed. "That's it, Don! That's it!"

I became excited to think of the many activities that I could now engage in. I wasn't wearing out; I was building up. So I shouted out, "Art! That's something that can be done just for the love of it, so it can bring beauty and enlightenment to the world. I could paint pictures and write books for no reason but to share my wisdom and make the world a better place."

Now I felt encouraged to come up with other things as well, so I noted, "I could take care of things. I could tend to a garden to help things grow. I could get involved in volunteer activities to make life better for others."

"Anything else?"

"Yes. I could work on my spiritual life. I'm afraid that my prayer life has greatly suffered because I've been upset with the possibility of aging and been too depressed and anxious to take the time to pray. I lost the reason to pray because I really didn't need anything. But that's not what prayer's for, now is it, Michael? Now I can see prayer as a way of being self-transcendent, of reaching out to God. My prayers are not for sending my list of needs and wants to God but for sending God the gift of myself. A prayer life that is appropriate for a healthy senior like me needs to be more contemplation and less supplication. I'm ready to focus on the God beyond me rather than treat myself as if I were God."

There was a prolonged silence between us. Then I broke the silence because there was one more thing bothering me. "Michael, what about those elderly folks who are frail or debilitated? Their poor bodies as so spent. Of what value is their advanced age in their condition?"

Michael looked at me as if to show how much he appreciated what I had just brought up. He stayed silent for a moment as he thought through his response. Then he leaned forward in his chair and said, "I think it was John Milton who made clear that those who wait can also serve. I think he may have been speaking of silent action, not inaction. You know, Don, with this in mind I must tell you it took me a long time to accept the value of a contemplative life. It seemed at first that, when people distance themselves from the everyday world, they are running from responsibility. But I have since learned that contemplatives who live behind gated walls in silence are not escaping reality but focusing deeply on it without the everyday distractions that tempt the rest of us all to live as if doing and getting and having were the prime virtues of our lives. They do not escape reality but escape these temptations so that they can concentrate on what remains—a life of self-transcendence and love. They are waiting yet serving.

"Don, that's how I see those elderly folks who are too debilitated to be externally active in the world around them. They can wait and serve. It's true that they're becoming more like infants as if to remind us all that they are progressing backwards toward their starting point. But since they are not infants, they can be internally active by praying and enduring suffering to prepare for their transition beyond this world and to selflessly offer these inner actions as gifts to make up for the faults and failings that surround them. And furthermore, Don, they can live as examples to the rest of us of patience and fortitude. I get a bit choked up when I imagine the scene of an elderly woman sitting hunched over in a wheelchair clearly crippled with severe arthritis being visited by a little child who gives her a flower. The woman tells the little one that she is so beautiful and precious, and that if she could, she would just scoop the little child up into her arms in a great big loving embrace. But for now she can only painfully reach slightly forward to gently touch the little girl's hand. That is what seniors who are debilitated can do—they can reach out no matter how slightly with an inner goodness and light that brings beauty and goodness to the world around them."

I was stunned. I could tell that Michael had reached deep within himself for his answer, and that the answer was spoken as much for his sake as mine. I could think of nothing to do but voice a heartfelt, "Wow." Then I stood up and walked over to where Michael was sitting. He rose to meet me face-to-face. With tear-filled eyes I said, "I want you to know how much I appreciate what you have done for me, Michael."

"What we have done for each other, my Friend. I have been touched as well."

I did not know what to do at this point, so I let myself go with the flow of joy and gratitude I was feeling. I reached out to Michael, put my arms around him and hugged him, patting him on the back as I did. He responded in kind, and when we separated, we looked at each other with warm smiles on our faces.

But I could not stay any longer because I had a new life to live, and it appeared that Michael felt the same way. So after I paid him for the session, I turned and walked toward the door. Opening it slightly, I looked back at Michael and he looked at me. I smiled at him again and I made a thumbs-up gesture to let him know that things were well, and I would be all right. He smiled back and enthusiastically returned the gesture. Then I left the room, but to this day I have not lost the feeling that captured my life in that room. I'm convinced that at my age I'm not only a treasure, but a gift for the good of the world and all that's in it.

Epilogue

A Table for Two at a Fine Restaurant

"So now you know where I'm coming from, Susanna, when I say I long to be with you to share my joy with you. There's no other reason. I hope you feel the same way. We can fill our lives with love for one another simply because we are with each other and are ready to make the world a more beautiful place. I'm different than I was before I got this old. I'm not as energetic nor frisky nor profit oriented. I feel a type of serenity like never before. So when I ask you to be mine, I'm not looking at what you can do for me. I'm looking at the treasure you are as you sit here before me, and I'm thinking about what I can be for you. Will you take me as I am, as I do you?"

"I do, Don" is all that Susanna says, but her broad smile and bright eyes say even more.

WORK CITED

All Scripture references are from *The New American
Bible*. Thomas Nelson, Inc., 1987.

ACKNOWLEDGEMENTS

Grateful acknowledgement is made to my wife, Mary Rose, who as collaborator and master editor fashioned my raw content into something that might engage and enlighten those who see fit to read it. I also want to acknowledge the kind work and vital insights provided by my readers, Victor Artigas, Barbara Goss and Ashleigh Jackson-Richards whose critique added crucial polish to this project. Lastly, I would like to acknowledge in this my Mary's and my 50th wedding anniversary year, it has been a blessing to live and love with my best friend and soulmate who has inspired me to write this book to help others find their own special place as they are getting older.

OTHER BOOKS
BY
ROBERT W. BAILOR

Passion, Longing and God, 1ˢᵗ Books (now Authorhouse), 1999, ISBN: 1-58500-585-1

A Month of Wonders, Authorhouse, 2006, ISBN: 1-4259-5623-8 (sc)

Chemical Addiction & Family Members (What Family Members Need to Survive and Thrive), Authorhouse, 2016, ISBN: 978-1-5049-6764-8 (sc), ISBN: 978-1-5049-6763-1 (e)

Through Fire to Faith (One Man's Journey from Fear and Fault to Genuine Faith), Authorhouse, 2018, ISBN: 978-1-5462-5532-1 (sc), ISBN: 978-1-5462-5533-8 (hc), ISBN: 978-1-5462-5531-4 (e)

Through Horror to Hope (A Faith Journey to Hopefulness in the Face of Evil), Authorhouse, 2019, ISBN: 978-1-7283-2874-4 (sc), ISBN: 978-1-7283-2873-7 (hc), ISBN: 978-1-7283-2875-1 (e)

Through Loss to Love (A Personal Journey to Discover the true Meaning of Life and Death), Authorhouse, 2019, ISBN: 978-1-7283-2968-0 (sc), ISBN: 978-1-7283-2966-6 (hc), ISBN: 978-1-7283-2967-3 (e)

All six books are available from authorhouse.com (1-800-839-8640)